Live life with joy!

Melanie Rock

The Lost Treasure Of Malta

Melanie Rock

iv

v

To my fellow Knights and Dames of the
Sovereign Order of St John of Jerusalem,
Knights Hospitaller and their commitment to
serving the Lord's sick and poor whoever they
might be. Especially to Sir Peter Leveque, Sir
Don Nicholls and my husband, Sir Daryl
Rock, who led to the creation of this story with
a casual conversation around a café table in
Malta, thank you.

Prologue

He dipped his pen in the inkwell to continue his entry. The light from the taper flickered and swayed as the ground shook throwing shadows over the stone walls of his home. Around him, he could hear the sounds of war. The tramping of armor-clad Knights on the roadway, the orders being yelled from commanders to soldiers, and the screams of the fallen. He could smell the dust raised by hundreds of feet, the sweat and stink of hard work and fear, and faintly, overlying it all; he thought he could smell the telltale coppery smell of blood that had been shed. He needed to finish this to take his place among the fighters. He was not one to shirk his duty, but his first duty was to document what he had done.

I write this as we are overcome and the once proud Knights of St John of Jerusalem surrender. And surrender we will. Unprepared we were for this despite the warnings which were brought to us by loyal men who, though there was great danger to their own persons, persevered through enemy territory, hunger, and great thirst, to bring us the knowledge of this invasion. If only the Grand Master had heeded their warnings. If only he,

Raphael de la Comte paused, there was nothing to be gained with reliving the past and nothing more he could have done to change the outcome of this day. When he had known in his heart that nothing would be done, he had broken his oath of loyalty. It had not been easily done. Many an hour he had spent on his knees, pleading with God to show him the way, to soften the hearts of the leaders, to find any other path to follow except the one of breaking his oath. His prayers had not been answered, and he had known what he must do. As shame swept through him at the memory, he tried to reason that in fact, his act had been one of supreme loyalty, of ensuring that the relics and treasures of the Order survived. And now, he had to make sure that these treasures would be found. He returned to his journal and finished his work. Quickly, he blotted the page and bound the book tightly in oilskins to ensure its safety.

"Jacques." He summoned his young page. Thrusting the package into the hands of the young lad, he said, "You know what you must do. Keep this safe at all costs and take it to my father." He laid his hand on the lad's shoulder. "Godspeed."

"Yes, my lord. You can count on me, sir." The boy stuffed the package in the pocket of his cloak, spun around and ran from the room, headed to one of the small boats that were going to try to make it off the island.

Raphael said a quick prayer of protection over the boy and the package. Then, after placing his helmet on his head, he picked up his sword and shield, prepared to do his duty.

1

"Jake?"

Jake wiped the sweat off his forehead leaving in its place a smear of dust and old cobwebs. The streak didn't mar his good looks. At 29 years of age he was tall and lean. A regular workout routine kept his muscles in good shape. He had never considered himself movie star handsome but more of the good looking 'boy next door' variety. His hair was naturally wavy and he kept it on the short side. His chocolate brown eyes were a great contrast to his blond hair and many women over the years had wanted his steady gaze to fall on them.

"Yes, Dad?" He tried not to let his exacerbation show in his tone but knew that he wasn't able to hide it completely.

"Are you finished yet?"

Jake snorted. Finished? He looked around the attic crowded with boxes, old trunks and old filing cabinets. Finished? When was the last time his dad had been up here? Finished was a long way off.

"Ah, not yet."

"Well, you must be hot and tired. Come on down, and we'll have a beer together."

"I'll be down in a sec. Thanks, Dad." Jake surveyed the piles he had already made. A small collection of keepsakes although heaven knows why he thought they should be kept. He figured that they were more than likely simply going to end up in another box back in the attic. A larger pile of stuff, for donations; clothes, lamps, old dishes, those types of things. Surely some church somewhere could sell that off at their bazaar as a fundraiser. And last but definitely not least, a bigger pile of garbage.

He started to gather up some of the keepsakes. He found that there were so many that he kept dropping them. Afraid they would break, he grabbed the closest box to use as a carrier. Covered in a thick coat of dust, he was dubious that the box would be strong enough to carry them. He pried off the lid. Moth-eaten blanket, definitely to the garbage pile, followed by a christening gown that was so old he wasn't sure it had ever been white as it was such a dark yellow color. He quickly considered an old pair of shoes, but the leather was too dry for even a couple of good polishes to resurrect them for the donation pile so garbage they were. Nestled in the bottom of the box was something wrapped up tightly and bound with a leather thong. Gingerly he pulled it out. It was relatively heavy given its size and looked as though it might be a book of some sort. He threw it onto the garbage pile and started to toss the other keepsakes into the box to haul down the attic stairs. Ready to head down for that beer, he hesitated beside the garbage pile, looked down and his curiosity compelled him to reach down and retrieve the package. He may as well give it a look before throwing it out. Maybe it was some first edition of some book and worth a small fortune. He snorted. Not likely but there wasn't anything to be lost by checking it before tossing it.

"Thanks." Gratefully, Jake accepted the cold beer from his father and took a big swallow to wash the dust out of his mouth and throat. "You and mom must have been storing stuff up there since before I was born! There are boxes and boxes and then more boxes of stuff."

His dad looked sheepish. "I guess I should have looked before I asked you to clean it out. I didn't think that there was really much of anything. I figured a few boxes of things like your old school report cards and a few keepsake clothes. Your mom always seemed to feel that some outfit of yours had special meaning and couldn't be given away. She must have stored a lot more than I had realized."

"No worries Dad." Jake tried to sound a lot more generous than he was feeling. Jake understood that his dad would have preferred to have been up there doing the work himself. Having to ask for Jake's help would have upset him. Since Jake's mom had died, his father's health had really started to deteriorate. Jake hadn't realized how much his mother had been taking care of until she wasn't there to do it. He could feel a wave of grief start to sweep over him. He pushed it away and concentrated on his dad. "I brought down a few things that I thought you might like to keep or at least look at before you throw them away."

Jake removed the bound package from the box and handed the rest to his dad. As his father started to empty the box onto the sofa beside him, Jake settled himself into the lazy-boy. Drinking his beer, he examined the package. It certainly looked old, but it also appeared to be in good shape. He gently pulled on the end of the leather thong, but the leather was too old and had dried into a permanent knot. He fished his Swiss army knife from his pocket and carefully sliced through the leather.

"What's that you've got?" His dad had finished emptying the box and had realized that Jake was looking at something else.

"I don't know. It was at the bottom of a box. It looks ancient and had been kept in this wrapper." Jake slowly unfolded the covering.

"That looks like oilskin. That is something you don't see very often anymore. I don't know anyone who wraps packages in it these days. Of course, now we have plastic to protect things. Back in the day, oilskin would have been the only choice to protect something valuable."

The oilskin had contained an old book, a journal by the look of it. The cover was leather and was embossed with Chevalier Raphael de la Comte. Jake very carefully opened it. The paper was crumbling around the edges a bit, but the pages had been sewn into the binding and not glued, so they remained in the journal.

The ink was surprisingly unfaded, but the handwriting was spiky and challenging for Jake to read.

"This Journal is the personal and confidential property of Chevalier R de la Comte, Knight Commander of Justice, Sovereign Order of St John of Jerusalem, Knights Hospitaller."

"What?" Jake's dad turned from examining the oilskin to give Jake his full attention. "Did you say Knights Hospitaller?"

"I did," nodded Jake. "Does that mean something to you?"

His dad sat back thoughtfully. "Funny," he said, "I always thought that my grandfather was making it up. But, I guess, given this journal, it must be true."

Jake waited.

"When I was a young boy, my grandfather would tell me stories about the Knights of Malta. He knew that I loved hearing stories of fighting and victories, the bloodier, the better at that time! Of course, when I was young, I had believed him, but as I got older, I assumed that he had made it all up to appease me. He claimed that his great great grandfather, was it three greats?" He waved his hand dismissively, "It doesn't matter. Whatever the relation, he had been a Knight of the Sovereign Order of St John, just like it says there on the cover." He gestured towards the journal. "And the name is a match as well. When I was older, I did a bit of reading around the Knights just out of curiosity. I assumed Gramps had done the same and used that information for stories. Anyway, they were a group of men from the aristocracy, usually the second and third sons who didn't have an inheritance and didn't want to be priests. The organization itself dates back to the Crusades in the Holy Land. The Knights made a name for themselves providing care to the sick and poor regardless of the person's wealth or religious beliefs. They were Christians but treated anyone: Jew, Muslim, or Christian.

They built one of the first hospitals in Jerusalem back in the early tenth century. As the Crusades ended, or in reality, as the Christians were driven from the Holy Land, the Knights were forced to abandon their settlements and hospitals and move. By that time, they had developed a branch or group of the Knights who were more soldiers than healers to help protect the overall group. The Order ended up moving around the Mediterranean for several generations until they ended up in Malta."

"Malta?" Jake frowned. "The only thing I know about Malta is that it had been a British military base and was heavily bombed by the Germans and Italians during the Second World War. I had no idea about the Knights."

"Given its central location, Malta has always been a strategic military outpost for all of the various empires that had sailed the Mediterranean, at least until airplanes could fly longer distances. The Knights were there for quite a long time. My grandfather told me stories about how they had resisted the Ottoman empire during a long siege. Other stories were about how they became renowned for their sailing and started raiding any Muslim ships in the Mediterranean. Of course, they justified that, using the fact that the Muslims were attacking Christian vessels as well. He told stories about the gold and silver and gems stones they amassed. They built forts and fortifications across Malta. Eventually, they were invaded by Napoleon, and that was the end of the Knights on Malta. Apparently, they have survived in a variety of ways through the years, but I can't tell you anything about that."

Jake was fascinated. He gently turned the book over and smoothed the cover. He wondered what the book had been through and how it had ended up in a dusty old box in their attic.

"My favorite stories were all about my great great great grandfather. He arrived to join the Knights at a young age but apparently was well respected. He was promoted through the ranks fairly quickly. My grandfather told a story about when the French arrived. It was full of intrigue and deception, just what I wanted to hear at the age of seven."

"What was it?"

His dad paused trying to remember the details. "The story was that the Grand Master, as they called their leader, knew that the French were coming. He either didn't want to admit he knew or figured that they would be able to fight them off as they had done with the Ottomans before. Or, I suppose, he could have made his own deal with the French. Anyway, your great great great grandfather couldn't stand by and do nothing. He knew that the French would take all of the treasures they had collected over more than 700 years. He got together with some other Knights that felt the same way. They tried to save as much of the treasure as they could in the short time they had. And of course, they couldn't be caught. That would have had terrible consequences."

"Why did they have to worry about being caught? It wasn't like they were stealing it."

"No, but in those days, you swore an oath of loyalty to the Order and the Grand Master. To go behind the back of the Grand Master and do something that he had expressly said not to do, well, it wasn't going to be forgiven."

"They took the things they could carry easily. My grandfather talked about how they would conceal things under their cloaks if they were small enough. They tried to take things of great value, but at the same time, they couldn't take so much that it would be noticed. Then they hid them. I don't know how long they had to be able to take things or where they hid them. My grandfather made up stories about how there was a secret map to the hiding place, but even the map was hidden. He would tell me these stories, and then, I would fall asleep dreaming of treasure hunting." He sighed. "I don't think I told my grandfather how much I loved those stories."

2

Jake scrubbed his hands over his face. Yawning, he stretched his arms over his head trying to relieve the strain in his neck and shoulders. He glanced at his watch. No wonder he was tired. He had just spent 4 hours trying to decipher the writing in the book. Not only had he discovered that the ink was faded in places, but the handwriting was not the best. The style of writing had been much more formal at the time, so it was also not an easy read. He had had to spend time here and there, reading and rereading to try to figure out exactly what the Knight had been saying. Of course, all things considered, he was grateful that it had been written in English. If Raphael had chosen Latin or French, it would have been useless. Carefully, he closed the book.

He leaned his head back, closed his eyes and thought about what he had read. It had made for fascinating reading. The book or journal, had given him a look through a window into a different world. A world that was completely foreign to him. One that he had never even known had existed before reading the journal. He had never liked history, and his school teachers had certainly not helped with that. His usual choice of reading material when he had been in school were the roadster magazines and occasional Playboy if one of his friends had been able to steal a copy from an older brother. His attitude toward history might have been a whole lot different if they had read this kind of thing when he was in school. Raphael hadn't written every day but tended to write about major events in his life. He wrote of his excitement when he had been accepted as a page to the Grand Master when he was just 14. He had run errands for him, carrying messages all over the island if necessary or taking packages to different watchtowers. Raphael had even documented his disappointment that as the Grand Masters had replaced each other over time, the importance of defending the island had changed. It seemed that slowly, there had been less and less concern about ensuring the safety of their home. The history of their success had led to complacency. While many watchtowers had been built, the Knight had been upset that the original number planned had not been completed. He was not sure if the ones they had would be sufficient to warn against invasion. Jake had learned that Raphael and his comrades were worried that the Order had lost its sense of purpose and was becoming more about power and money than serving the Lord's sick and poor. It seemed that they had grown unconcerned about the threat of the Ottoman Empire.

Jake hadn't quite figured out the entire timeline, but he was beginning to get a feel for the ebb and flow of the conflict between Christians and Muslims. But services to the sick and poor had been a core part of their organization. Committing to that had apparently been a part of their vows when they joined the Order. He had read about Raphael's rise in the Order from page to Knight to Commander of Justice and so on up the ranks. As he had risen, he had worried that the Knights' service to the people was becoming less and less important. Towards the end of the journal, Raphael had written extensively about his anxiety that the Order was no longer prepared for outside threats. He felt that the internal politics of the higher-ranking members had become a matter of exceeding importance to them. Jake sighed, thinking that some things never changed. It seemed that if any organization was around long enough, it ended up mired in politics and power struggles.

The end of the journal was the most interesting. Raphael had described pretty much exactly what his father had told him earlier. How a small group of his most trusted friends had banded together with him to try to protect the heirlooms of the order. They had believed that the French were coming and that the Order no longer had the courage or the military might to withstand their invasion. They had been horrified when the Grand Master... Jake carefully flipped through some of the final pages; ... Grand Master von Hompesch, had dismissed the warnings of the incoming spies.

Jake reread the passage.

Sir Joseph von Rechberg arrived today. He has lost a great deal of flesh and looks old beyond his years. He spoke of days of hiding from French forces with little to eat or drink. He has traveled from Austria and through Italy. He had left Italy by boat but calamity struck shortly after they set sail and the French had overpowered their vessel. Sir von Rechberg was wounded, but in his wisdom, was able to keep the documents from harm. As evidence of God's great grace, the captured were set ashore in Civitavecchia. The affidavits he carried have revealed beyond doubt that the French will invade. The great General Napoleon is setting out for Egypt and taking Malta on his way is key to his success in Africa. I and others are horrified by Grand Master von Hompesch's dismissal of the threat. How can he be so blind to the ways of the French? Can he not see the overwhelming ambition of Napoleon? The need for Napoleon to make himself the greatest general of all time? And with that need, the cost. He is desperate for money to pay for the wars that feed his ego. The few of us who tried to bring sense to the Counsel were unable to overcome their self indulgence and sense of security. I fervently pray that God will reveal the truth to him and other members of the Counsel before it is too late. May God's will prevail.

Further on, Jake had found reference to the treasure and his ancestor's role in what became of it. He was fascinated by the risks they took.

Today I have broken my vows and with that my heart. But, I have chosen to follow what I believe to be right and not that which my vows dictate I should do. I, and those who are like-minded, have agreed to save what we can. Without a doubt, the French are coming. Without a doubt, they will strip us of our treasures. The desire for gold seems to be the curse of all mankind. We refuse to see our offerings to God and the Order be used for war. We will keep from harm only a little, and my heart aches that much of what

I would have chosen to save is either too large or would be missed. May God understand that this act is to honor our Order and Him. It is not an act of selfishness or disrespect.

I will give this journal to my page to carry to my family in England. I pray that he will find his way safely. This journal will be the map to the relics of our order. Find below direction to the place of concealment. As I fear that the lad will not survive our enemies, the instructions are not plain but when understood, will guide one to the whereabouts. I pray that this book will be kept from enemy hands and only those who are loyal to the Order will find that for which we sacrifice much.

Jake had skimmed the rest of the journal, but it had meant little to him. As he sat there, he wondered what they would have hidden. He knew that relics in the church often meant the bones of some saint or a piece of wood purportedly from the Cross or the ark or something. But he wondered about the mention of treasure. Had they stashed away some gold and silver? Would it have been coins? Maybe they had hidden plates and candlesticks or silver cutlery. He began to think about the Knights hiding the things they had pinched. He envisioned them collecting the plunder and what, riding off with it? Burying it? Throwing it into the ocean to be retrieved later? This whole thing was the plot of a movie or a book. Knights and Generals, hidden treasure, clues to its location. How much better could it get?

He laid the journal on the side table. It was incredible that the journal had not been opened and read before he had done so today. Had it not been delivered to the family of Raphael de la Comte? But, it must have been delivered given that Raphael was apparently an ancestor and obviously the journal had been passed down through the generations. What had happened to Raphael himself? Had he been killed in the invasion? Had he never made it home? Jake marveled that the book had survived and had even travelled across the Atlantic when his great grandparents had emigrated to America. He shook his head as it was spinning with all that he had learned and with all the unanswered questions. With the romantic idea of a treasure hunt to fill his dreams, Jake took himself off to bed.

3

Rachel Corbyn barely caught the papers as they started to slide off the pile of books and binders she was juggling. She wondered yet again why doors had to be so difficult to get through when one had no hands free. She leaned to one side and used her elbow to push the lever down and her hip to push the door open. The papers almost went over the edge again as she shifted to get through the opening. She absolutely needed to get a briefcase.

She climbed the stairs and repeated the exercise to get out onto the third floor. As she entered her office, she dumped the load onto her desk. Colleen, with whom Rachel shared her office, smiled.

"You had best be careful. Not much more will fit on that desk of yours. You really should clean it every once and a while."

Rachel plopped down in her chair and swiveled back and forth. The chair squeaked. Getting oil for the chair, another thing to add to the ever-growing list of stuff she should be doing. She shoved her glasses up her nose and rested her head on the back of her chair.

"I know, I know. But cleaning my desk seems like such a waste of time. Besides, I know where everything is even if it is a mess." She scanned the desk piled high with books and papers, unanswered message slips and somewhere, under the pile there was a phone. Maybe. "Okay, I sort of know where everything is. Besides isn't that a sign of a good historian, too busy digging up information to clean her desk?"

Colleen laughed, "Okay, that's good. I haven't heard that before. I'll give you that one."

Rachel turned around in her chair and gazed out the window. Since she had journeyed to England to do her PhD in history, she had always been struck by the irony of the view out her window. Cambridge University was the second oldest university in the English speaking world and yet all she could see out her window was the chrome and glass building across the grass which housed the Faculty of Divinity. Even the Faculty of History building within which her office was located, had been built less than 50 years ago and was an architectural example of brick and mortar. Somehow, she felt that given she had travelled over 3500 miles to be there, she should really be able to see some of the old ivy covered stone buildings that had existed for hundreds of years. She swung back around and glanced the clock on the wall.

"Dammit, is that the time? I'm supposed to meet Gregory five minutes ago. He hates when I am late and he makes sure that I feel his displeasure!"

"He pretty much hates everything unless it is young, willing and female," said Colleen snidely. "I don't understand why you have him as your thesis advisor. Wasn't there anyone else that you could have asked?"

Rachel agreed that her thesis supervisor was not her favorite person. He always made her feel like she was somehow small and inconsequential. In his presence, she felt that he thought she didn't know anything and couldn't be expected to produce any work of any value. His attitude seemed to border on contempt but not enough that she was able to have anything to report to his superiors. She figured it had been like that for years. His reputation for misogyny was well recognized although it wasn't openly discussed or dealt with by the university. She assumed that was due to a combination of him never quite stepping over the line and the University not wanting to have to deal with an ugly situation. However, concern about his superiors did not keep him from working his way through the wide eyed, worshiping, new female undergraduates every year. The University continually turned a blind eye to those wholly inappropriate relationships.

She gathered up the papers she needed to take to the meeting. "I'm too old for him to be interested, so that isn't a problem. And he is the expert at this university on organizations like the Order of St John, the Knights Templar and the Freemason's. No one else here would have been the slightest bit interested in my work. Gotta run." She headed for the door.

"Good luck," Colleen called out after her.

Rachel raced down the hallway and up one flight of stairs. As she got to his office, she took a deep breath. She never liked to show him that she had rushed to get there. As part of her defense against his belittling attitude, she felt she needed always to look like she was in control. She shoved her blouse back into the top of her jeans trying to straighten it out.

She rapped sharply on the door.

"Enter."

"You are late."

Gregory Bothell, or Dr. Bothell as he insisted he be called, sat leaning back in his beautiful leather chair behind his beautifully polished and neat antique mahogany desk. She was sure that it never saw more than 2 or 3 neatly stacked pieces of paper on its gleaming surface. While Rachel had forgotten to touch up her lipstick after lunch, was sure her hair was falling lopsidedly out of her ponytail and felt sweaty and rumpled all over, he appeared relaxed and untouched by the realities of life. Relaxed and untouched, she added silently to herself, in a very expensive suit. Rachel shoved aside the faint feeling of resentment that came from knowing that she had been working all day as his teaching assistant as well as trying to fit in her own research and writing while he sat unstressed and unfettered in his beautiful large office. But that was the difference between the life of a tenured professor and the life of a Ph. D candidate. The latter was the life she had chosen for the moment.

"Have you forgotten that you requested this meeting? That I adjusted my schedule to accommodate you?"

Right, you probably had to move your tennis game to later in the day, Rachel thought. She squelched her irritation. Letting it show would only result in making him much harder to deal with now and in the future.

"I am so sorry, Dr. Bothell." She tried to inject the correct amount of contriteness into her tone. "Elizabeth from the History of Greece class is struggling with her paper. I spent more time with her than I should have."

He waved her apology away. "Then you need to manage your time more efficiently. You are here now, so what is it that you wanted to speak to me about?"

As she hadn't been invited to sit, Rachel very tentatively perched herself on the front edge of a chair across from him. He made no comment, so she relaxed a bit and started searching through her papers.

"You know how there has always been talk that the Knights of St John knew in advance that the French were coming but did nothing about it? Well, I have been doing some reading in the Archives of various journals that were kept by scholars and monks in the time shortly after the French invaded Malta. Most of it has nothing to do with the Order and is just about their daily lives and what they did and ate and that sort of thing." She saw him frown and hurried on before he could say how uninterested he was in all of that. "But I found this one book that had been written by someone as his memoirs and apparently, he was at one time a page to one of the Knights. He didn't write the book until he was very old but he wrote about his time in Malta and the coming of the French. Specifically, he wrote about the fact that his master and a group of other Knights tried to get the Grand Master to prepare for the French, and when they couldn't, they started to take the treasure the Order had collected." She paused for breath.

"Really, Rachel, you think that a Knight is going to break his vow of fealty to the Grand Master to steal a few pieces of gold. Loyalty was their touchstone. The most important feature of the Order. Loyalty to the Grand Master and then to their fellow knights." He sat up and shook his head. "Rachel, my dear girl, if you haven't yet learned that at this point in your thesis, I think that you are having more problems than you are admitting."

Rachel ground her teeth at his patronizing tone and the 'dear girl' comment. She knew better than to address it. It would only mean that he would use it more often or worse, come up with a more degrading term.

"I know that, sir, but the page writes about the fact that he had been given a book to take to England to give to the family of the Knight. He says it contained the directions to the hidden treasure." She hunted through the pile on her lap again. "Here, I photocopied the relevant pages in the journal. It is hard to read but look at it."

He slid his reading glasses onto his nose and accepted the paperwork. Leaning back again, he began to skim the text. As Rachel watched, she saw his eyes sharpen and then narrow ever so slightly. Finally, she thought, I have his attention. I have shown him that I know what I am doing.

He sat back up and threw the papers onto his desk.

"All this is, Rachel, are the ramblings of an old man who is about to die and is worried that he will be forgotten. He was simply looking to make a name for himself. There is nothing here to suggest that any of this actually took place. He is clearly making it up as he writes. You would be best to ignore this and move on in your research."

"But, Dr. Bothell, I looked him up, and he was a page to the Knight

Raphael de la Comte. He was there around the time the French invaded, but there is no record of him after that. He simply disappears, until this journal. He isn't listed on the list of prisoners the French took. And there is no mention of him becoming a Knight when he got older. So, what happened to him? The only explanation is that he left the island before the French rounded up the prisoners."

"Rachel, again, you are allowing your feminine romantic nature to cloud your vision as a historian. He was likely imprisoned when the French took over. The names of prisoners were rarely seen as worthwhile to record. Or he was killed. Or, he travelled with the Knights as they dispersed. As a page, he wouldn't have been important enough to have been noted in the records."

Once more, she ground her teeth at the reference to her 'feminine nature'. Determined not to allow him to shut her down, she persevered. "But, the French took over the island with very little resistance and almost no fighting. They took very few prisoners, preferring to simply allow the islanders to continue on with their lives. If he had travelled with the Knights, why isn't there a record of him becoming a Knight? After all, the purpose of becoming a page was to gain admittance into the Order as one got older. And he couldn't have been killed given he wrote the journal years later. And this journal wasn't found on Malta, it was found....I think....". She trailed to a halt. He had unceremoniously held up his hand to stop her.

"Stop Rachel. Forget about this issue. Move on to research that is more central to your thesis. Stop wasting your time on ideas that are merely figments of some old man's imagination. Now," he stood up, "I have another meeting. Please see yourself out."

Rachel could feel that her face was flushed and her heart was pounding with frustration. She wanted to yell at him that he was a stupid fool and couldn't he see that this was an incredible opportunity. That if this was even remotely true, they needed to follow it up. Fuming, she turned smartly on her heel and left. It wasn't until she was almost back at her office she realized that she had left the papers on his desk.

4

"Tricia, are you scheduled to be the one here overnight?" The vet assistant smiled and nodded at him.

"Yes Dr. C."

"Please make sure to keep a close eye on him overnight. And call me if anything happens that could mean a problem." Wearily, Jake pulled the OR cap from his head and untied the mask from around his neck. It was nearly seven o'clock, and he had been at the office since just after six this morning. His days in the OR didn't usually go on for so long, but just as he had been about to pack up and go home, an upset woman with her even more distraught young son had rushed into the office carrying their young dog. He had been hit by a car and was badly injured. Jake could have required her to take the dog to the emergency clinic but the dog was clearly dying, and if the bleeding wasn't stopped quickly he was going to die. The sight of the young boy with tears welling up in his eyes but trying not to cry while holding onto the puppy's front paw as his mother cradled the pup, was enough to have Jake scooping the dog from the mother and ordering his staff to set up the operating room for an immediate emergency exploratory surgery. He had been able to get the bleeding stopped and luckily there were no serious internal injuries. His hind leg had been severely broken, but it had been a clean break, and Jake had taken the risk of using plates to hold the bone together in the hopes that it would heal properly. He had thought at one point about simply amputating the leg which would have been faster, easier and less likely to cause complications but the memory of the young boy's big eyes pleading with him to save his dog had him trying the more complicated procedure first. He headed out to the waiting area.

The mother and the boy were the only ones there as the clinic had already shut for the day. The mother hopped up from her seat immediately when she saw him, but the boy simply wrapped his arms around his legs tighter and shrank back into the chair.

Jake smiled at the mother. "What's your son's name?"

"Brian. How...."

Jake sat down beside him. He spoke directly to him.

"Hi Brian, I'm Dr. C, what is your dog's name?"

A small tear stained face looked up at him. "T-t-tigger."

"Well, Tigger has just had a big operation, but he did well coming through it. He has a broken leg that I have tried to fix. He is going to need a lot of love and care over the next few days, but I am hoping that he will do well. He is going to have to stay here for a while, but you can come and visit if you want." The little blond head nodded vigorously up and down. "Now, you should know that his broken leg may not heal properly so he might have to have another operation later. I am hoping that I won't have to do that. For now, he is asleep, and he will be that way for a while. Do you want a visit before you go home to bed? It will have to be a quick one because he needs his sleep to heal up."

Again, there was a vigorous nod.

Jake led him and his mom into the back of the office. Various sized cages held everything from meowing kittens to full-size Labradors to a couple of ferrets. Tricia was just about to close the door to Tigger's cage after checking to make sure his IV was dripping properly. When they entered the room, she turned and smiled at them. Leaving the door open, she gestured for the young boy to come closer.

"He is sleeping, but he can hear you. You can pet his paw and tell him how much you love him."

The dam of tears broke as he reached for his puppy's paw. "I'm sorry Tigger, I didn't see the car, I didn't mean for you to follow after the ball. Please get better Tigger; please get better." He laid his head against Tigger's and cried. Tricia looked at Jake with a pained look and then crouched down beside him. She put her arm around his thin little shoulders. She spoke softly to him, trying to comfort him.

Jake turned to the mother who was now weeping silently.

She sniffed back her tears. "Brian was playing fetch with him in the front yard, and the ball took an odd bounce out into the road. Brian yelled for Tigger to stop but he is still just a puppy, and he didn't listen. There is a reason why we called him Tigger! The car didn't have any opportunity to try to miss him at all. Brian has been feeling so awful; like it is all his fault. I tried to tell him that accidents sometimes happen, but he is such a sensitive boy."

Jake was doubly glad now that he had made an effort to try to save the leg. At least, assuming everything went well, there wouldn't be a three-legged dog to constantly remind the boy about the accident. The mother put her hand on Jake's arm.

"We don't have a lot of money but please do what you need to do to fix him. I will pay whatever it costs even if it takes me a while. I just can't stand to see Brian so broken by this accident."

Jake shook his head. "Don't worry about the cost; we can figure something out. I just hope that the fracture heals properly. There is still a chance that I may have to amputate the leg. I used a plate and several screws, but if it doesn't knit together properly, it may need to come off."

She closed her eyes and then opened them again to gaze at her young son. "I understand. Thank you for everything that you have done. Brian, we have to go now. Give Tigger a kiss and tell him we love him. Tell him that you will come back and visit him again as soon as he is awake and you are allowed to."

Brian kissed the dog and gave him one more gentle pat. He turned and ran to Jake to fling his arms around Jake's waist and squeezed.

"Thank you, Dr. C. Thank you for saving my dog."

Jake showed them out and then returned to finish up the documentation on the puppy.

"Good night Tricia. Thanks. Let me know if anything happens. Oh, and by the way, make a notation on Tigger's chart that we are only charging our costs. No additional fees at all."

Jake turned up his coat collar against the freezing wind and slogged through the slush of another east coast winter. He had always loved having the change of seasons but winter seemed to have started a bit early this year. He slid into his car and slammed the door. He was pretty sure he could sense more snow coming. He closed his eyes and rested his forehead on the steering wheel. He had been working twelve hour days now for weeks. Ever since one of his partners had had a heart attack and had to be off work for six weeks, Jake had been working overtime. His partner was due back next Thursday. Jake was more than ready for him to come back. The practice had multiple partners, but Jake had taken on the majority of his partner's patients as the two of them did most of the surgical cases within the group. Thursday, he would be back Thursday. Jake decided as he slid his key in and turned the car on, that next Friday would be an excellent time for him to take a holiday. Maybe a quick trip to Florida for sunshine and warm weather. He could cancel his upcoming appointments and move anything urgent to the returning partner given his schedule had not been booked pending his return. Then, he thought of the small book which lay on his bedside table. The journal had been nagging at him ever since he read it the first time and he must have reread it four or five times by now. Yes, he was due for a holiday and Malta was just the place to take it.

5

Blearily, Jake handed his boarding pass and passport to the smiling Air Malta attendant. The attendant's smile brightened even more as she looked over the handsome passenger. He had apparently been traveling for a while and was a bit crumpled, but that couldn't take away from the good looks and great body. She liked the way his blond hair curled over the back of his collar. He wore what seemed to be the American uniform of jeans and a t-shirt. She had no idea why Americans didn't realize that dress pants and an attractive sweater could make any man look sexy and successful. But still, for him, she would make an exception. She added a bit of invitation to her smile. After all, she had time to kill on her layover in Malta. He smiled in return, accepted his passport and headed onto the plane. She shrugged philosophically and turned to the next passenger. There was always a next passenger.

Jake had been traveling now for what seemed like two days, but he knew in reality, it was only about eighteen hours. The flight from New York to London had been delayed for a couple of hours which meant he had to catch a later flight to Malta. However, as he stowed his carry-on, he was grateful that there had been a later flight. Spending the night in Heathrow had no appeal.

It had taken only a couple of days to sort out the details, cancelling his upcoming appointments and surgeries, arranging for his partners in the clinic to cover his on-call shifts and ensuring that his dad would look after his cat. He had dropped her off at his father's place on his way to the airport along with her food, litter and her seemingly endless array of cat toys. As usual, she hadn't been the least bit upset he was leaving her. As long as there was someone to feed her, cuddle her and play with her, she was a happy cat. Tigger too, had done exceptionally well and had been more than happy to go home with an even happier little boy. Jake felt his heart swell a little as he remembered. He didn't think that he had ever seen a pet and owner so ecstatic to be reunited. The entire office had spilled out into the waiting room to watch the reunion. And these were the same people who had been shocked that he was going away. He had been a bit offended by this. He didn't think that taking this trip was so much out of the usual for him. Yet, as he sat there, he couldn't remember the last time he had gone on a trip which hadn't been to a conference, and even those were few and far between. He was the one who took the extra shifts and did the coverage for the other vets as they went away with their families. Maybe this was a bit out of character for him, but if it was, well, so much the better. It was time he started to enjoy his life a bit more.

He settled himself into his seat. If he were lucky, he could catch a few moments of sleep on this flight.

"Excuse me," Jake looked up. A gorgeous young woman with a tentative smile was gesturing towards the inside seat. "That's my seat."

"No worries," Jake popped up, feeling a bit more energized now that he knew he would have an attractive seatmate. "Can I help with your carry-on?"

She clutched what appeared to be a brand new briefcase to her chest. "No thank you, I've got it." She awkwardly made her way into the row and sat.

Jake resumed his seat. He extended his hand. "Hi, I'm Jake."

He looked at her, appreciating the view and making no effort to hide that he liked what he saw. She was tall and slim. She had long honey colored hair which she wore straight down with a few bangs to soften the cut around her face. She was wearing glasses that were not apparently adjusted properly, as she kept having to push them back up her nose. Jake found it endearing. She turned and looked at him. Blue, he thought, big, blue eyes, no not quite blue, more a green-blue he decided. He saw them become more guarded as she noticed his appreciation of her. She looked at his hand and slowly moved hers to take it.

"Hi."

Her hand was small in his but her grip was firm.

Jake kept a hold of her hand, and asked: "And you are?"

Rachel tried to pull her hand away from his unobtrusively. Unsuccessful, she sighed and gave up. "Rachel. Can I have my hand please?" He slowly released it.

Not put off by her unfriendly greeting, he persisted in trying to engage her in conversation.

"This is my first time to Malta. Have you been before?"

"No."

She settled her briefcase on the floor in front of her and adjusted her seatbelt.

Jake tried again.

"What takes you there? Holidays? Work? Although, quite honestly, I'm not sure what they do on Malta. Anyway, I am going for a vacation. A bit of sunshine and adventure to break up the routine." He broke off to smile at the flight attendant making her final check through the cabin.

Typical, Rachel thought noticing him smiling at the attendant. Lots of empty seats beside other women, families and clearly uninteresting men and I have to end up with the handsome schmoozer who is ready to turn his charm on any woman in his vicinity. Irritated, she felt she needed to put him in his place.

"Tourism and Trade."

"What?" Jake was taken aback. He pulled his attention from watching the very fine back of the attendant walk up to the front of the plane to frown at Rachel. "What did you say?"

"Malta's economy. It depends on Tourism and Trade, and on manufacturing as well."

She pulled some paperwork out of the briefcase, pushed her glasses up her nose again and started to read.

Jake gave up, leaned his head back and was asleep before they had taken off.

Rachel couldn't concentrate on what she was reading. It wasn't important for her to read anyway as it had merely been a way of shutting down her row mate. Given he was now sleeping, it seemed to have worked. She dropped the papers into her lap and looked out the window. The engines revved as they barreled down the runway and the ground fell away beneath them. Rachel felt the plane bank as it continued upward.

Well, she had done it. After the last humiliating meeting with Dr. Bothell, she had been stewing about what to do. Finally, one night after lying awake again for what seemed like hours, going over and over her research and her encounter with Dr. Bothell, she decided that it was time for her to take action. The next morning, she had gone to his office to inform him that she was going to be taking a few days off, maybe two weeks. She had concocted what she thought was a reasonable excuse and wasn't an outright lie, in case he demanded an explanation. She knew that she would never be able to sustain a blatant lie if he started to question her about things in more detail. She was delighted to be informed by the department secretary that Dr. Bothell had taken a three-week leave of absence and was unavailable. Rachel had told the secretary that she was going to be away for the next two weeks but was reachable by email. She did not disabuse the secretary of her apparent belief that Dr. Bothell was aware that she was going to be away. Feeling slightly guilty, she rationalized that she hadn't been asked outright if he knew. It wasn't her fault if incorrect assumptions were made.

Then in a flurry of activity, she checked to make sure her passport was up to date, had arranged coverage for her teaching assistant work, (she would owe Colleen for that one), gathered all the documentation she felt she would need, went online to book her flight to Malta, and stuffed some clothes haphazardly in her suitcase before heading to the airport the next day. A bubble of giddiness rose up inside her as she remembered the chaos she had created. She couldn't remember the last time she had done something so spontaneous and, some would say, irresponsible. The bubble threatened to erupt into outright laughter. Maybe, she thought, it was high time for her to have done this, and maybe, she should do it more often in the future.

At 25 years of age, she had spent all of her time studying history and not really living it. Her knowledge came from books and papers, not from visiting places and seeing the marks left by those who had come before. She had been so focused on completing her PhD that she had never taken the time to experience different parts of the world. Even since arriving at Cambridge, she had not spent any time exploring the area. She rarely strayed from the campus. She would have to change that in the future. Visiting places and having context would help her interpretation of history and enable her to portray it more realistically. She sighed, rested her head back on the headrest and closed her eyes. She acknowledged to herself that up until this point, she had been so focused on getting her BA, then her Masters and now on completing her PhD that travel hadn't even really been on her radar. Of course, it wasn't like she had tons of money to go jetting off all around the world. But, like this trip, she would have to make it work.

6

Jake stepped out of his hotel into the bright sunshine. He could feel the heat of the sun through his clothes and was grateful for the cool breeze off the water. He had slept later than he had anticipated and so wasn't off to as early a start as he had expected.

"Good morning, sir."

"Good morning. Which way to Valletta?"

The doorman pointed up the hill. "Just to the left at the top of that hill, sir, you will find the main gate into the city." He turned to gesture down the hill towards the water. "Of course, you can walk around by the water that way but you will enter through a side entrance, and it is quite a bit further away. If this is your first time to Valletta, I would recommend you use the main gate. It is quite impressive. If you would like, we could have the hotel car take you up." The doorman reached for the phone to call the driver.

Jake stopped him. "No, that is quite alright. A walk will do me good. Thank you." Jake nodded to the doorman and slid his sunglasses on.

He slowly walked up the stairs to the main road, enjoying the cheerful displays of bougainvillea and hibiscus. He had chosen a hotel which was on the waterfront. It was a beautiful hotel and a lovely spot. But it did mean that it was located at the bottom of the hill upon which Valletta, the main city of Malta, had been built. He didn't mind the climb, though. It felt good, after the previous day of being scrunched into airplane seats, to be able to stretch his legs. He continued his climb up the road toward the main gate at Valletta. Being mindful that the traffic moved in the opposite direction on the road than he was used to, he took his time in crossing the road. True to the doorman's word, as he reached the top and turned to the left, he could see the walls of the city rising upwards and the main gate open and welcoming. As he neared the gate, he walked through parked taxis and horse drawn cabs. The horses stamped their hooves impatiently and shook their heads to rid themselves of fat, buzzing flies. Small booths appeared along the sidewalk, offering meat pies and the traditional Maltese morning pastry, the pastizzi. His guidebook had informed him that he should not leave Malta without having experienced the cheese and pastry delight.

As he came around the side of a booth, the city lay before him. The gates were no longer there, and the drawbridge had been replaced by a stone walkway. Still, he was struck by the size of the walls of Valletta. He paused at the side of the path to take in just how thick the walls were. The pale yellowish orange of the limestone blended in with the surrounding land making the city look as if it had simply grown up from the ground. He could see where the limestone of the walls had eroded in places and where the city had unquestionably made some restorations. An agile feral cat picked its way along the side of the wall, walking on what looked like an impossibly small ledge created by the erosion. He stood and absorbed the atmosphere, the feel of the sun on his face, the heat that was starting to increase, the dusty smell of the stone, and the crowds of people making their way into and out of the city. He thought he could pick out the tourists from the locals. The former with their shorts and running shoes and their cameras slung over their shoulders. The latter were on their way to work in business clothes, suits and dress shoes or dresses with heels even in the heat.

He continued into the city. The road, for while it may have been a drawbridge in the past, it was truly a road now, bridged the vast moat that ran around the city. It was, of course, empty of water and he could see cafes and restaurants starting to be developed on the floor of the moat. He was pretty sure that the moat had always been dry and was used as a line of defense to make it difficult for oncoming enemies to reach the walls unseen and unopposed. And, if one thought about it, it made sense to increase the height of the walls, not by building up but by digging down. Jake assumed that in digging out the moat, much of the rock would have been used to build the walls. He passed between the high walls into the city proper. The main road stretched before him down the hill. It was filling up with people; some in a rush with places to get to, many just sauntering and enjoying the day. His stomach growled to remind him that he hadn't eaten since sometime yesterday.

When he had finally arrived at his room, he had been too tired to contemplate more than splashing water on his face, giving his teeth a quick brush and falling into bed. Now, he was ready for coffee and breakfast. He could see several sets of tables and chairs up ahead. As he approached, he noticed his seatmate from the plane had already found the same café. He had discovered last night, as she checked in ahead of him, that she was staying at the same hotel.

Now, she was sitting alone, a partially eaten croissant, an empty coffee cup and her guidebook on the table.

"May I?" he gestured at the nearby chair. Without waiting for her answer, he sat.

"Can I get you another coffee? We seem to be destined to run into each other. I figured that means we should get better acquainted. Besides, I'm here alone, and you appear to be here alone and having breakfast with someone is so much better than having it by yourself." He glanced through the menu for the Café Royale. He got the attention of the waitress. "An Americano, please, as well as a plain croissant."

He gestured to Rachel who was staring at him with a mix of horror and disbelief. She couldn't believe that he had had the audacity to simply sit at her table without waiting for an invitation.

"Would you like another coffee?"

"No, no thank you."

Jake stretched his legs out and crossed his ankles enjoying the sunshine.

"So, Rachel, what brings you to Malta, tourism, trade or manufacturing?"

Rachel looked at him sharply, unsure of his motives and flustered by his abrupt appearance. She was used to being approached by men, but generally, her reserved manner and unfriendly expression were enough for them to get the message and leave her alone. But despite how she had treated him yesterday, here he was, smiling and relaxed, offering to buy her coffee. She wasn't quite sure what to think. Good manners overcame her wariness.

She returned the smile cautiously. "Okay, I deserve that. I wasn't overly friendly yesterday. I'm not a good flier, and that makes me cranky." She took a deep breath. "I'm here on holidays I guess."

"All is forgiven." Jake paused to be served his breakfast. He sat up and ripped apart his croissant. Rachel watched with envy as he smeared butter followed by jam thickly over a piece. He looked at her quizzically before popping the morsel into his mouth. He closed his eyes in pleasure as he chewed. "Oh, you have to admit, the Europeans absolutely know how to make the best pastries."

"They aren't afraid to use butter. That's why everything is so good." Rachel couldn't help but smile at his obvious enjoyment of his breakfast.

Jake's eyes popped open, and he started to prepare another piece. "But why 'holidays I guess'? Usually, trips are divided into holidays, business, conference, family visit or a mix. Either way, people usually know why they are traveling."

Jake saw that he had gone too far as Rachel's expression froze. She began to fumble with her purse, trying to get out her wallet and to slide in her guidebook at the same time.

"Yes, well, I'm on holiday. It was just an impulse decision, so I haven't spent a lot of time thinking about it." She counted out her euros and tucked them under her cup. "Well, thanks for the company."

She pushed back from the table and threw her handbag over her shoulder. Her chair was set to rocking violently by her rapid turn to leave the table.

"Something I said?" Jake said to the empty air left by her speedy exit. He shrugged and turned back to his breakfast. While her rude departure had irritated him somewhat, he refused to allow it to affect his day or his enjoyment of this most excellent croissant.

He had decided to take the first few days to explore the city of Valletta as it had been the center of the Knights' domain on the island. After he was more comfortable and had more local knowledge, then he thought he would start to try to figure out the meaning of the clues in the journal. Glancing through his guidebook, he decided that he would visit the hospital first. After all, it was a hospital which had been the genesis of the Order.

He finished his coffee and paid his bill. After asking the server where the hospital was located, he decided to take the longer route to get there. He slowly walked down the main road. Crowded with people, it was a busy pedestrian mall. However, as he narrowly escaped having his toes run over, he realized that while the main road may be car free, the side streets were not. Cars and trucks made their way across the boulevard with little regard for the pedestrians. Having a close encounter with a horse-drawn cab taught him that they were worse in terms of caring about pedestrians. The cabbies called out shrilly to warn those walking as they wove through the streets at a trot. Given that they neither slowed nor gave way, they apparently expected to be heard and heeded. Jake listened to the clip-clop of the horses' hooves and thought about what it must have been like when the Knights had lived there. Horses for the Knights, horses for drawing carriages and carts. Stalls and shops would have lined the streets, not unlike they were today but filled with necessities as opposed to tourist baubles, clothes, and jewelry. Merchants would have been calling out their wares, trying to attract their clientele. Thinking about it realistically, he reckoned that the air would have been full of the smell of manure and sewage. Given the Knights' predisposition for cleanliness, he wondered how they dealt with the reality of no sewage system. Or did they only worry about cleanliness at the hospital and left the city to fend for itself? Jake made a mental note to see if he could find out.

Jake tried to take in all the sights around him. He found that he often had to stop and look up. The buildings rose two to three stories above him. The height of the buildings and narrowness of the streets meant that most of the street was in the shade at any particular moment during the day. Only when the sun was directly overhead was it uncomfortably hot. Keeping the streets narrow and the buildings relatively high was a conscious design intended to maintain a cool comfort in the city. The only exposed areas were the squares which were dotted through out the city. They had served as gathering places for the populace. Many of the buildings had shops below and apartments on the upper floors. Most of the apartments had small conservatories built out slightly from the building, more as 'Juliet' balconies than real balconies. They were framed in wood which had been painted a dark green. Many of the windows were open. Bright flowers hung from window boxes competed with fluttering laundry for the little sun filtering down.

Other buildings were built entirely of stone. As he walked, Jake was able to identify the Auberge de Provence which was apparently now a museum. He wasn't quite sure what an Auberge was, but he was sure he would find out at some point. He passed the Co-Cathedral of St John. He stopped to read the signs outside the cathedral but was unable to find any reference to why it was called the co-cathedral rather than just a cathedral. Another puzzle for another day. He was surprised at how plain and unpretentious the Grand Masters' Palace appeared. It certainly didn't follow the European standard for palaces. It had no gilt or gold and was simply a square building built out of the same ubiquitous rock. Nothing marked it as being particularly special except for the crest and inscription mounted on the side commemorating the presentation of the St

George's Cross to the people of Malta. The dates showed that this had happened after the second world war. He decided he would visit both of the palace and the co-cathedral later.

He continued down Republic Street and found that the road suddenly got a lot steeper. He could see Fort St Elmo at the end of the street, identifiable by its thick limestone walls zigzagging around the buildings in the centre. As he reached the walls of the fort, he turned right and made his way down the road towards the Malta Experience. Here, he would have his tour of the hospital.

He purchased his ticket for the tour, which included a movie, and followed the guide into the theater. The theater was about three quarters full. In the dimness he could just make out the long honey hair and tell-tale glasses of Rachel. He slid into the seat behind her.

"I'm not following you, you know." He spoke into her ear. She started and turned to look at him. Jake was unable to interpret her expression in the gloom of the theater. Anything she was going to say was pre-empted by the movie and music starting. He sat back and adjusted his earphones to the English translation and watched the movie. The movie provided him with a synopsis of Maltese history. Much of it was about the devastation of World War II but there was also some information about the Knights. Jake mused that for a small island, it had been through more than its fair share of major events.

"Right this way please," requested the Maltese guide, gesturing to the group to move through the gift shop and up the stairs. Jake wasn't sure if Rachel was purposefully putting space between them or she just happened to be the fastest in the group as she darted on ahead. "You can come back to the gift shop after the tour. Please stay together."

The guide spoke with an accent that Jake was unable to place. It wasn't English or French or even middle eastern. Whatever it was, it was easy to listen to, and she evidently knew her history. She led the gawking tourists up the wide stone staircase and down the hall. Suits of armour stood at attention at intervals along the way. Jake stood beside one. The Knights had been considerably smaller than he was. At least the one who had owned that particular suit of armour had been.

"Here, we are in the top hall of the hospital." She gestured down the room. "This is the Sacra Infermeria, and it is 508 feet long. This hall was the central ward of the hospital and admitted the Knights and the wealthy of the island. You will notice that along the walls are niches built into the walls. Between each of those niches would have stood a bed. Each of those beds would have had one of the niches assigned to them. That was the toilet. Which is a fancy way of saying a hole in the floor through which the waste would drain."

A quiet titter of laughter ran through the group. The guide smiled in appreciation.

"The toilet would have been covered with a drape to provide some semblance of privacy. Under usual circumstances, each bed would have had one patient, and only one side of the hall would have had beds. In times of an epidemic or war when there were more patients requiring beds, they could then line both sides of the room with beds. On this floor, there would be no more than two patients per bed even during the worst of times." She paused. "Any questions so far? No, then let us continue. The hall downstairs is the same size as this one. It was for the poor. There, they were not so lucky as to have their own bed and toilet as they had to share two to a bed. If there were lots of patients, then it could have been up to four per bed. Each bed would still have had their own toilet."

She walked them a little farther into the hall. "If you look up higher on the walls, you will see elongated openings cut into them. On the other side of that wall, there would have been a garden planted with orange trees and lemon trees and other plants. The scent of that garden would have drifted into the ward to keep it smelling fresh. Patients who were well enough could have visited the gardens if they wished. There are no windows other than those openings which made it easier to keep the room cool in the summer and warm in the winter."

None of what the guide was saying was new to Rachel. She had learned this all a long time ago. She tuned her head and looked around the hall. She could picture the beds lined up along the wall, the drapes hanging in the niches. Knights would have been moving from bed to bed to care for the sick and wounded. The faint smell of oranges would have hung in the air masking the smell of disease and sickness. She thought about how lucky the people who had had the ability to access the Knights' care had been. The care they would have received would have been far better than any of what Europe would have had available to them at that time. She wondered if they even realized how privileged they had been.

The guide continued. "The Knights were well renowned for their effective treatment of patients. Drapes were used above the beds to identify at a glance what the diagnosis for each patient was. A green curtain, for instance, might have signified an injury, a blue one perhaps, pneumonia. They were ahead of the actual understanding of bacteria and viruses as infectious agents, but they understood that sick patients could spread disease to other patients. Rather than have contagious patients in the same ward with the others, where they might pass cholera on to the Knight who was in with a broken leg, they were segregated to an area for infectious patients. Any patient who had been diagnosed with a contagious disease was sent to the quarantine area rather than left to infect the rest of the patients. All the patients were served on silver plates with silver cutlery. Silver, we now know, is very antibacterial in its properties. They would not have known that specifically but again, they recognized the fact that those who ate off silver, were sick less often than those who did not. They treated open wounds with honey which, again we now know, is too sweet to allow bacteria to grow and thus prevented infection. And they used a guillotine to amputate limbs which reduced the damage done to the flesh on the part of the extremity which was still attached. It also meant that there would have been minimal bleeding due to the speed at which the procedure was carried out."

She started to move back towards the exit. "In those days your skill as a surgeon was based on how quickly you could amputate a limb. For most surgeons, the fastest they could do it would be three to four minutes as they would have to saw through the arm or leg. Sawing through bone takes a bit of time. The Knights were able to guillotine off a limb in no more than nine seconds. As you might imagine, that was likely much more tolerable."

Jake saw several shudders pass through the crowd and had to admit that the vision of having someone saw through his arm or leg was not a happy one. He followed the group back down the stairs into another room directly below the main hall. He caught up to Rachel as they climbed down.

"It's a pretty gruesome thought isn't it, having your limb cut off with no anesthetic." Jake tried to engage her in conversation. Rachel barely glanced at him.

The tour guide gestured towards the walls. "You will see embedded in the walls here the occasional metal ring. Those are left over from when this was the police stables. The transformation into stables happened long after the Knights had left. In the time of the Knights, this would have been the ward for the poor. Now keep in mind, they only admitted male patients. Women were not cared for at the hospital."

"That is the end of the tour. Thank you for coming. I hope you enjoyed it. If you have any questions, I would be happy to answer them for you. I will stay here for a few minutes."

The group all said their thanks to the guide and a few eager ones clustered around her to ask questions. Jake made his way outside. Blinking in the sunlight, he retrieved his sunglasses from his pocket. He scanned the scattering tourists. Rachel was already walking down the hill away from the hospital. He shrugged and wondered why he was such a sucker for punishment. He figured that she wouldn't be very welcoming, but he started off after her anyways. There was something about her or maybe it was the challenge of overcoming her unfriendliness, that drew him to her.

As he walked towards her, he saw a smartly dressed man approach her. She stopped abruptly, plainly not pleased to see him. Jake could see him give a formal nod of the head to her, followed by what appeared to be an angry comment from her. He shook his head and held up both his hands as if fending off her anger. Rachel turned on her heel and started striding away from the man and back towards him.

Jake waited for her to draw abreast of him and then fell into step with her.

"Who was that? Someone you know or is someone trying to bother you?" Jake looked around to see if he was following them, suddenly wondering if the man had been a well-dressed stalker. He could not see him.

Rachel's face was set in angry lines, but telltale tears leaked from her eyes. She dashed them away with the back of her hand.

"He makes me so angry."

"Come here." Jake placed a guiding hand on her elbow. He felt her momentary resistance and then she acquiesced. He looked around and spied a street side café. He guided her over and pulled out a chair.

"Here. Sit."

He gestured to gain the attention of the waiter and ordered a glass of water and white wine for both of them.

She slumped in the seat across the small table. "I knew I couldn't trust him. I just knew it."

She took a deep breath and started to speak, the words tumbling over each other in her hurry to get them out.

"I am a Ph.D. history student working on my thesis. So, this is sort of a working holiday as my thesis is about the Order of St John."

Jake became more alert. "Really. You must know a lot about the

Order and the Knights. I would have thought that you would have been here countless times."

The wine and water arrived. Rachel attacked her glass of water like it was alive and drank it down. When it was empty, she more gently returned it to the table.

"I'm sorry, I just don't know what makes me angrier. The fact that he makes me angry or the fact that I let him get under my skin every single time. I swear he works to make sure he irritates me every time I see him."
She looked at Jake. "Sorry, what were you saying?"

"I said that I thought you would have been to Malta before given your thesis is about the Knights. I was just surprised that you hadn't been."

She laughed bitterly.

"Funny enough, I have read just about every old and modern book that exists about them, and I have spent countless hours in museums and archives trying to piece together their history and separate fact from fiction, but this is my first time on Malta."

Jake played with his wine glass. "I have only just come to know about the Order and the Knights. I can't say I know very much about them but what I have read is fascinating. I am particularly intrigued by the way they just seemed to give up when the French arrived. They had so many years of history as a force to be reckoned with and then, poof, suddenly, it's over." Suddenly realizing that her understanding of the Order would be miles ahead of his, he was worried he might have offended her with his assumptions. "Of course, I don't know very much, and for all I know, they did put up resistance or fight."

Rachel's face relaxed a bit. She took a sip of her wine and leaned forward, her forearms resting on the table. "No, no, you are correct, and you have just stated my thesis topic. Why after so many successful battles and having such a successful military history did they simply allow the French to walk in and take over? Was it simply the wrong Grand Master at that time? Was it that the Order has simply lost its way? She paused. "Why with their network of spies over the continent, did they not know about the arrival of the French? Or if they did, why did they ignore it? Did they ignore it? Was the approach taken with the French agreed upon by all of the Knights? Did any of them dissent?" She colored slightly. "Sorry, I can go on a bit about the Order. I find them fascinating, but I know not everyone does."

Jake smiled. "Please, go on. It is always a pleasure to see someone who is so passionate about what they do. By the way, who was that man?"

Rachel's face suddenly froze. Her smile disappeared. Jake could practically feel her draw herself back into her being.

"That is the high and mighty Dr. Bothell."

Jake was shocked at the degree of anger in Rachel's voice. He looked at her in surprise. She was clearly distressed; her hands were tightening around her wine glass until he was worried she might snap the stem. Her knuckles were white, and she had developed two bright red spots high on her cheeks. He laid a comforting hand over hers.

"Okay, and who is this Dr. Bothell? For someone high and mighty, I haven't heard about him." He said attempting a joke.

She was slowly relaxing her grip on her glass, and her color was returning to normal.

"I'm sorry." She looked away from him, clearly embarrassed at her display of emotion.

"Rachel." He grasped her hand. "It's okay. Just tell me who he is and why you got so angry."

"HE makes me angry. I take him the information I found about the Knights knowing about the French, and I take him the rumor I found about some of the Knights trying to save some of the treasure, I tell him all of these things because he is my supervisor. Because I am supposed to tell him things, and he is supposed to help me put my thesis together. And what does he do?"

Jake waited.

She took a breath, "He tells me about how I have it all wrong and obviously my information is incorrect and that I need to go back and look at it again. I need to find independent corroboration. That I can't use unsubstantiated information in my thesis, especially not for this type of situation. And then what? He takes my information from me, and now, he is here, he is in Malta. A place he has never expressed even one iota of interest in coming to, but no, all of a sudden, he is here. On vacation. When was the last time he took a vacation? Usually, he just hangs around the department not doing anything but taking all the credit for everyone else's work." She suddenly recollected herself. "Oh, Jake, I am so sorry. I didn't mean to go all psycho female on you. You must think I am an idiot."

Jake quickly assimilated all the information. "Not at all. And I think I've got it. That slick, smarmy dude is your supervisor for your thesis. You shared information with him about a possible hidden treasure, he told you to ignore it, and now he is here, and you think he is after the treasure. Did I get that right?"

Rachel stared at him in astonishment. "That pretty much sums it up. Why are you not laughing about how stupid an idea it is?"

Jake hesitated. "Because I don't think it's a stupid idea."

Glancing at his watch, he stood up and held out his hand. "How about some lunch?"

7

Early the next morning, Jake sat on the waterfront at his hotel. Sipping his coffee, he enjoyed the view. Yesterday had been a beautiful day he decided. After the run in with the irritating Dr. Bothell, as Jake had named him, they had enjoyed a leisurely lunch, lingering over a bottle of Prosecco and excellent pizza. He had ended up spending the rest of the day with Rachel. They had wandered through the streets doing some window shopping and people watching. Despite their rocky introduction, they had fallen into an easy way with each other, pointing out things of interest or joking about the tourist uniform of shorts, runners and camera. Nothing more had been said about the incident with Dr. Bothell. He was beginning to think that she was just the person he needed to help with interpreting the journal, but he had shared nothing of it yesterday. She had been so upset after the professor that he had tried to distract her from it. Then, after a while, he had completely forgotten about it as they had enjoyed a light dinner and talked about nothing important. Well, he would talk to her later but right now he wanted to see if he could figure anything out.

Jake pulled the journal towards him and gently opened it to the page he had previously marked.

With great bravery comes wisdom, sometimes to flee, sometimes to hide is honor. May the very ground in which we stand lead to that place of honor.

Well, he certainly hadn't been terribly descriptive with his clues, thought Jake. As a map it left a lot to be desired. After all, weren't treasure maps supposed to have instructions like 'go ten paces west and look for the bent tree' and an 'x' to mark the spot? He was beginning to doubt his ability to decipher this written map. What had seemed like an easy task when he had been reading in his living room at home now looked like an impossible feat. Malta seemed so small yet was so large with history and monuments, with stories of war and glory as well as great compassion and kindness. Maybe the best thing to do was to talk to Rachel. Jake shook his head, annoyed that he was ready to give up before even really trying to decode anything. He wasn't even sure of his motives for wanting to ask her. Was it because he wanted to spend more time with her or because he needed the help? He had certainly enjoyed their afternoon yesterday. He had discovered that she was doing her studies at Oxford, but she had grown up in in a small town in Maine. That had explained the lack of an English accent. More importantly, he had learned that she had a great sense of humor and while she didn't smile very often, when she did it lit up her face and turned attractive into beautiful. Yup, he thought, I'd be just fine spending some more time with her whatever the reason.

Let's break it down into manageable pieces, he thought. With great bravery...where would they have shown bravery? Jake carefully unfolded the map of Malta he had picked up in their wanderings yesterday. Bravery would have been a result of a war, mostly likely. But then again, he thought, maybe it was bravery against disease and pain. In a time when there were few treatments for disease, caring for the sick and dying often meant the caregivers themselves also got sick and died. Looking at the map, he identified the forts the Knights had built. Fort St Elmo at the foot of Valetta and Fort St Angelo across the harbour were easily identified. But then were there not forts at Birgu and Isla as well? Or was that Victorriosa and Senglea? And what about Selima? He couldn't see a fort marked on the map at Selima, but it seemed funny that they wouldn't have had something on the point. It was directly across the bay from Valletta so one would think that it was a prime location for a fortification. And of course, there was Valletta itself. AND if he included the disease angle, he would have to include the hospital.

He could feel his excitement starting to be extinguished by the weight of the reality of what he had undertaken. Could he figure things out? And even if he did, would he be able to find the next clue? Would that clue even exist still? He had learned yesterday that Malta had been extremely hard hit during World War II with several thousand tons of explosives being dropped on the island and extensive damage had been done. Could what he was looking for have been destroyed or buried under tons of limestone rubble?

Not yet prepared to give up, he tried to give himself a bit of a pep talk. He needed to focus on the process of doing this, the fact that it gave him a focus for exploring Malta as well as learning more about his family. The history that he had never known. So what if he got nowhere? It was still a holiday and a fun experience. Resolved, he took on the next section of the clue. *Comes wisdom*. Well, that would certainly fit with the hospital. The Knights had been ahead of their time in knowledge of disease and treatment. But, as he thought about it, it was knowledge that they had at the hospital. He didn't see wisdom as being the same thing. Wasn't knowledge information based whereas wisdom was more experience based? Deciding that he had to start somewhere in terms of winnowing down the choices, he decided that he would work with the definition of wisdom as being experience based.

So, if that was the case, it would make more sense that the bravery referred to was from fighting. Great, so that narrowed it down to seven possibilities.

Sometimes to flee. Jake's knowledge of the Knights' history was a still a bit sketchy, but he couldn't think of a time that they had fled except before they had come to Malta and then with the invasion of the French.

To hide is honor. Jake couldn't understand that. He couldn't reconcile the Knights' reputation with them also hiding. Honor, Jake gazed thoughtfully out over the harbor. Honor, where had that come up before?

Jake closed his eyes, lulled into a doze by his jet lag, the warm sun and peaceful surroundings.

"Good morning. Am I interrupting?"

Jake started, coming alert quickly and almost dropping the journal as he sat up straighter in his chair.

Rachel stood next to the empty chair across from him.

"Can I join you?"

"Absolutely." Jake tried to close the journal carefully and at the same time keep it hidden from her view.

She pulled the chair around to face the harbor view. "It is so gorgeous here. So much history." She turned to look at him and gestured to the journal. "What is that you have? It looks pretty old."

Casually, Jake slid the journal down the side of his chair. "Oh, this, it's nothing. Nothing much at all, just an old book I was looking at."

Rachel looked embarrassed. "I'm sorry, I didn't mean to be nosey. It looks old, so it's a historian's curiosity to ask."

She recognized that she could be pretty nosey at times. It had always been her biggest flaw, and her mother had told her a million times that people didn't like it when she asked too many questions. She sat in the chair beside him and tried to relax to enjoy the view.

They sat looking out over the harbor with what Rachel took to be an awkward silence between them that she didn't understand. Yesterday afternoon, it had been like they had known each other for years. Of course, crying and getting infuriated tended to break down barriers pretty quickly. Rachel tried to make conversation to ease the tension.

"It's an impressive view of the city from here. You have some of the older city buildings and the more modern condos that have gone in. Then there is the contrast between the fishing boats and some of those big yachts that are moored across the way." She paused, not sure he was listening. "It's an interesting statement on old and new. Don't you think?"

She realized that the discomfort she had been feeling had been entirely one sided. Jake clearly hadn't been paying any attention at all.

Jake hadn't been listening to her but abruptly realized that she was waiting for a response. He had been thinking about the journal and the fact that he had made no progress at all in understanding it. He was unrealistic if he thought that he was not going to need help with this puzzle. He just didn't know enough. Here was a great resource sitting beside him. He would be foolish not to use it.

"Rachel, I need your help." He pulled the journal out from between the arm of the chair and his leg. "This book is a journal, written by my great great great grandfather, or is it my great great great great grandfather? Anyway," Jake waved a hand dismissively, "That doesn't matter. What matters is that he was a member of the Order. A relatively high ranking member." Jake watched in confusion as Rachel's expression changed. She seemed to go from happy to disbelieving to angry. Jake didn't know why.

Rachel couldn't believe it. She felt like the ground had shifted underneath her feet. Here was someone in whom she had confided her biggest frustrations and fears. And what had he done in return? Hidden from her who he was and why he was in Malta. Hidden it behind an innocent exterior, pretending to be interested but all the while knowing more than he had let on. Rachel felt a flush rise to her face as she thought about how she had shared information with him thinking that he wanted to learn. Apparently, she was a sucker and a bad judge of character.

"Seriously, you have been telling me for two days now how you don't know anything about Malta or the Order, how it is all new to you." Her voice started to rise in anger. "And now you tell me that you have this book, this journal, that probably says more about the workings of the Order than anything that I have read. Seriously, did you think I wouldn't notice, or that I wouldn't care? What were you planning on doing? And to think that I told you about the hidden treasure. Stupid, what a stupid thing for me to do." Her voice hitched, and she could feel tears forming in the back of her eyes. "You are as bad as Dr. Bothell."

She practically spat out the last sentence and pushed back from the table so quickly her chair overturned. She turned to go furiously blinking back the tears. She wasn't going to cry; she wasn't going to let him see how upset she was. Let him think that she was just angry. That would be good, but she didn't want him to see how much she was hurt.

Jake looked at her in genuine confusion. "What are you talking about?"

Suddenly, he could see how the situation looked from her side. She had told him all about her circumstance and he had said nothing about his. She obviously thought that he had been hiding it from her.

"No, please," Jake stood and put a restraining hand on her arm, trying to stop her from stalking away. "No, it isn't like that. Please, sit down, let me explain."

Rachel hesitated still fighting the tears. She looked at Jake. His expression showed that he was feeling ashamed and upset because he had upset her. She looked at the journal. It was clearly extremely old. It appeared to be in very good shape all things considering. Her curiosity warred with her sense of betrayal that she had been lied to, that she had been somehow manipulated. Her curiosity won. She righted her chair and sat down but only after pointedly moving the chair several inches away from his.

"Fine, explain."

"First of all, I am sorry. I didn't mean for you to think that I was keeping anything from you. It's just this really is all new to me, and

I'm not sure what to make of it. I only found the journal several weeks ago when I was cleaning out my dad's attic. It was then that he told me that his grandfather had told him stories about the Knights and about their history. My great grandfather seemed to have focused on the bloody fighting times, but I suspect that was because that would have been what my dad as a kid would have wanted to hear. But Dad never told any of those stories to me. I have never heard of the Knights or the Order until after I found the journal. I wasn't even planning on coming to Malta until about two weeks ago. I was tired and fed up at work and needed a break. Malta seemed like a good place to go. Besides, you were so upset yesterday that I didn't want to add to your stress. I didn't even think about it really. Please, I am sorry."

He looked and sounded sincere. Rachel chose to believe that what he was saying was true. She nodded tentatively.

"Okay, I believe you...for now. Will you tell me about what's in the journal?"

Jake told Rachel about how his great great great great grandfather had been one of the Knights alive during the time of the French invasion. That the Journal recounted how a group of the Knights were unhappy with how the Grand Master was handling the situation. He told her about the fact that the same group of Knights had foreseen that things would not go well for the Order and that they had come together to try to save some of the relics and treasures of the Order. He told her of how his ancestor had shared his struggles with his conscience and sense of duty in removing and secreting away the treasures. How he had felt it was a breach of his oath but that he felt more strongly that he needed to follow what he knew to be right.

He came to the end of the story. "He struggled with doing this but was so sure that it was the right thing to do that he did it anyway. The group of them were worried that if the journal was found, the treasure would be too easily found if they simply gave directions. So my great great great great grandfather wrote clues that apparently guide you step by step to the treasure. I can't believe it is still hidden and hasn't been found, but when I decided to take a holiday, I couldn't resist the idea of coming here to look. I'm not this kind of guy usually. I am usually pretty boring."

Rachel was looking at him with a brilliant smile. Her eyes were alight with delight. "This is a fantastic find you have. It could answer a lot of questions. And, it confirms my theory. I can't believe that the treasure would still be around to be found, but it is certainly worth looking for." She was practically dancing in her chair with excitement. The sense of hurt had been erased by elation. "And it would be fun."

Jake placed the journal on the table between them.

"I've been sitting here trying to work out the first clue." He related to her what he had already thought about. "But, I don't know enough to be able to understand anything else about it. I thought maybe you could help."

Suddenly, a thought struck him.

"Wait, I know where I've seen him use honor before." Quickly he started to flip through the pages, slowing down as some of the edges flaked away. "Here, at the end of the entries. He talks about how hiding the treasure is about honor."

Rachel asked, "Are you willing to let me look at the journal?"

Jake briefly hesitated and then chiding himself for his hesitation, he handed it to her.

"The first clue is where that bookmark is."

Rachel noticed his hesitation in giving her the book and inexplicably she felt a small stab of disappointment that he still didn't trust her. She wasn't sure why it should bother her, after all, she had only just met him, but for some reason, she was hurt that he had hesitated, even if only for a split second.

She accepted the journal and stroked the cover almost reverently. She was actually holding a piece of history, a book that a Knight had handled and written in, had recorded his innermost thoughts. For her, the journal in and of itself was a treasure. She could barely believe that such a book existed and whether or not their treasure hunt turned anything up, she would never forget this moment.

Carefully, almost reverently, she opened it to the bookmarked page.

"Let's get to work."

Hours later, Rachel set her coffee cup down with a bang. The bang was an expression of her frustration.

"We have been at this for hours, and I still don't have any ideas." She blew her bangs up in frustration. "All I know is if I have any more coffee, I am going to start shaking."

Jake had already given up and had moved to one of the lounge chairs to get more comfortable. He lay there with his hat over his face to protect him from the sun.

"Come over to the dark side." He patted the lounge chair beside him. "Come and lie down for a while. Maybe lying down will get more blood to your brain and help with ideas."

Rachel grudgingly got up from the table. She always hated to leave something unfinished. She lay back and stretched out.

"Um, this is pretty nice."

She could feel the warmth from the cushions seeping up into her back and shoulders helping to relax the knots that had formed as she had hunched over the journal. The sun beat down upon her. The cool breeze feathered across her body, keeping the sun from being too hot

"Isn't it, though? How often do you get to do this?"

She closed her eyes against the sun. "Not nearly often enough. Did you remember to put sunscreen on?"

"Who needs sunscreen? Besides I am rarely in the sun. And I need my vitamin D!"

"You should always wear your sunscreen anyway. Don't you know that? Of course, you aren't as fair as me. I always turn red, burn, blister and peel. I end up right back at the pale white I started at."

"Umm."

Figuring that was the end of the conversation, Rachel allowed herself to soak in the sunshine. She concentrated on feeling the coolness of the breeze as it passed over and the feeling as it ruffled her hair. She felt the roughness of the fabric of the lounge chair as it pushed against her shoulders. She could feel beads of sweat starting to form on her lower back. She absolutely needed to do this more often. So much of her life was spent running from one appointment to the next. She would plan her day down to the minute in order to know when she was going to be able to do some of her research. She had so many teaching commitments that it ate into her own thesis time. She had let her self-care slide. Lying here like this, she couldn't remember the last time she had done yoga or even gone for a walk. All of her walking seemed to be running between buildings at the University. She resolved to change that when she was back at work. Somehow she had to figure out how to make herself a priority.

When she was back at work. When this was over. Whatever this was, holiday, treasure hunt, research expedition, it had barely begun, and she was thinking about the end already. Jake. She had barely met him and yet they had embarked on this crazy hunt together. She thought about him. He clearly took good care of himself. His shoulders filled out his t-shirts very well as far as she was concerned. His leg muscles were well-defined runner's legs. She knew he was a runner because the shirt he was wearing advertised a half marathon from last year. All in all, he was one very good looking package. Slightly guiltily she wondered about what was waiting for him back home. A job, obviously, a girlfriend, or maybe a wife, children? She realized how little she knew about him. But, she also acknowledged, how much she would like to get to know more about him. Deciding that it might be a good idea to think about something different, she turned her thoughts back to the journal.

She lay there letting the clue run through her mind. And may this ground in which we stand. She bolted upright, "That's it! Jake, get up." She shook his shoulder. "Are you asleep? Come on, get up."

Having been enjoying a wonderful state of doziness, not quite asleep but not quite awake, Jake wanted to ignore her voice. Another shake of his shoulder emphasized her impatience.

"Jake."

The intensity of her tone cut through his doze.

"Alright, alright, I'm up. What is it? This had better be good." He had the foresight to mumble the last comment to himself.

Rachel was back at the table, "Look, Jake, what would you typically say about ground and standing?"

"Um, that we are standing on it."

"Exactly, we are standing on it, but that isn't what he says."

Jake tried to concentrate, still feeling dopey. He sat up hoping that would help. "It isn't?"

Rachel rolled her eyes impatiently, "No, it isn't. Here read this." She practically shoved the journal into his hands.

"May the very ground in which we stand..." he trailed off as she interrupted.

"Don't you see? The ground in which not on which, in which."

Jake was trying to keep up. "Okay, but isn't that just a difference in what they said then and what we say now?"

"No, I don't think so. The Knights had tunnels under all of the forts. They used them for storage and for safe places they could retreat to in times of siege. If they were under siege, the Knights may not have been able to return to their Auberges, their dormitories." Jake checked Auberges off his list of things he needed to know and added tunnels instead. "They would be stuck in the fort so they would sleep in the tunnels while others kept watch. That way if there was an attack, they would be safe and able to continue to rest. During World War II, the Maltese used these tunnels and even expanded the tunnels to allow the population on the island to live underground at night. The Allies used to have their center of operations underground, in the so-called Churchill tunnels."

Jake was finally cluing in, "So you think that by saying in the ground, he meant the tunnels." Jake's spirits started to lift. "That would fit with the part about fleeing or hiding; the tunnels would be where they could flee or hide if they needed to."

Jake jumped up from the lounge chair. Grabbing Rachel, he led her on a dance around the pool.

"We did it; we solved the first clue!" He stopped suddenly almost overbalancing Rachel. "But, if there are all these tunnels under the city and on the island, how will we know where to look?"

"The Great Siege of Malta happened before Valletta was built. The Order was on the other side of the bay in the Three Cities and Fort St Angelo. Valletta wasn't built until after that time. The odds are that when he spoke of hiding, he was referencing the period of the Siege. I think we should look there."

"Okay, but where is there?"

"The tunnels are mostly under the Military Museum which is in Birgu." Rachel whirled around in his arms. "Birgu is right there" She was pointing across the bay.

Jake suddenly became aware that he was still holding her. His arm was tucked around her waist, and she was leaning back slightly against his chest. He was struck by how well she fit. Suddenly uncomfortable, he quickly dropped his arm and stepped away. "Well then, I guess it is off to Birgu."

Oblivious to his reaction, Rachel started to laugh from excitement and happiness. "Come on; we have to go look!"

8

After consulting with the concierge about the best way to get to the Three Cities, they started off down the hill. There were ferries making the crossing at regular intervals.

Rachel was positively bubbling, and Jake could only hope that her enthusiasm was seen simply as an eager tourist. As they waited for the ferry, he idly scanned the tourists around them. People watching was often a great source of entertainment. Tourists certainly came in all shapes and sizes. While there were still some who carried a large camera around their neck or over their shoulder, he noticed that most of them seemed to be using their phones. That reminded him that he hadn't been in touch with his father since he left. He made a note to try to send a quick email to his dad that evening. There was also the odd person who was wearing clothing for cooler weather. Jake assumed that they were likely locals. One, in particular, was wearing a jacket as well as a heavier hat. Given the heat, he certainly seemed overdressed for the weather. But, he had a large camera around his neck, and Jake thought maybe he was a local playing tourist in his own town. He was distracted by Rachel pulling on his sleeve.

"Come on; the ferry is here." She led the way, paying their fare and then clambering up the ladder to the top deck. Jake would have been happy to sit in the back, but Rachel pulled him up to the front.

"What an incredible view you get of everything." She exclaimed.

As the ferry pulled out from the dock, they sat and enjoyed the ancient city of Valletta and the three cities. The sunshine gleamed across the water turning it into a vivid aquamarine blue. It bleached the limestone of color so that walls of Valletta appeared almost white. The contrast was breathtakingly beautiful.

Rachel leaned over the railing and pointed out Fort St Angelo. It was located on the tip of the Peninsula. Birgu, which was where they were headed, and Senglea were two of the three cities. Rachel told Jake how after the Great Siege was over they had been renamed Citta Vittoriosa and Citta Invicta for their roles in the Siege. The 'Malta at War Museum' was just on the outskirts of Birgu.

The ferry docked along side a brick pathway that paralleled the bay. Once they had disembarked, Jake doubled checked the map to ensure they headed in the right direction. With a crowd of other tourists, they made their way up the hill towards the fortifications. They had at one time served to protect Birgu but were now protecting the War Museum.

They entered a courtyard through an arch built into a four-foot thick wall. The courtyard was square and dominated by a staircase that led up to the ramparts. There, along the wall and pointing out to sea were several cannons. Rachel carefully picked her way up the steps to the cannons. The stairs had a rise of only two or three inches and were about six inches in depth. They had been worn in places by contact with the many pairs of boots that would have been up and down them over hundreds of years.

"I assume these stairs are cut like that to let them get the cannons up and down the battlements." Jake awkwardly walked up them. The constant wear had also polished them to a shine and made them quite slippery. "I would not have wanted to be one of those guys trying to get one of those suckers up that so called ramp." He looked at the cannon which was approximately nine feet long. There were five of them. "Nope, I would have found something else to do that day."

"Imagine what it must have been like to stand here and see hundreds of ships sailing towards the island and into the harbor. Hundreds of enemy ships."

Rachel could picture it. The soldiers on duty on the wall, likely complaining about how hot they were in their armor, drinking water and watered down wine. Perhaps playing dice and not paying attention until the horizon took on a fuzzy dark shade. That fuzzy line would have gotten bigger and bigger, and then they would have been able to make out the individual ships. She wondered if they had had a telescope. Telescopes had been valuable instruments and often only high ranking officers had been allowed to use them. But surely on watch, someone must have had something to be able to see into the distance. Once they realized that the fuzzy line was ships, many, many ships and enemy ships at that, the cry would have gone up. She could imagine the activity that would have broken out around her. The sentries coming to full attention. The alarm being sounded across the Fort and the surrounding villages. The villagers would be summoned into the Fort for their own safety. As the ships would have taken some time to reach a point of being able to cause damage, they would have had time to load up their carts with food and animals and bring them to the fort. They would have wanted to be inside the fort before the doors were closed and barred. Ammunition stores would be checked and double checked, and the power for priming the cannons would have to be brought up to the wall from the powder room. Preparations would have been made for ferrying more gunpowder and cannon balls to the cannons as needed.

The kitchen staff would have been checking stocks and ensuring that the Fort had enough water and food to withstand a siege for some time. Hopefully, they would have done their jobs before the arrival of the ships and done it well. Then the waiting would have begun as the ships got closer and closer. The Great Siege involved forty thousand enemy soldiers. The ships required to carry that many would have stretched as far as the eye could see. How intimidating that must have been. Did any of the ships come in close enough to fire against the fort or did they simply bide their time waiting just beyond reach? Was the original plan to under take a siege or had that simply been a result of not being able to over come the defenses of the Knights? Rachel wondered who made the first shot. She pictured the bustle around each cannon. Each soldier knowing and performing his job as part of a unit.

"Imagine it, Jake. It took twelve soldiers to man each cannon. One would swab the cannon, then one gunner would prime the cannon, load it with powder, stuff in a wad of paper and then another soldier would ram it down. Then others would aim the cannon. Another gunner had to ensure that the was sufficient powder at all times and another soldier was in charge of maintaining the cannon balls. The noise would have been deafening, the air full of smoke and powder. The cannons would get hot, and the soldiers could easily burn themselves while loading them. Of course, once they settled into the siege, there wouldn't have been a lot of firing as the enemy would have stayed just out of range. Only if they thought they could gain an advantage would they have approached the walls."

As she described it Jake could see the groups of men huddled around their own cannon. Doing their jobs despite the heat, the noise, the smoke. The villagers huddled together in fear and anxiety. Children crying, wives anxious about husbands who may not have made it in from the sea or the fields before the gates were closed. Overall, Jake was very glad that he had not lived during that time.

"Time to go, Rachel, if I let you, you will be here all day reliving the past."

Her face creased with her beautiful smile. "That's part of what historians do. Great historians can make the past come alive."

"Then you must be a great one. Come on."

As they carefully made their way down the stone steps, a shadow caught the corner of Jake's eye. He stopped and looked again, but there was nothing to see. While he and Rachel had been reliving the past, it looked like all the other people had entered the museum. He shook off an uneasy feeling that the shadow meant something. He followed after Rachel. At the reception, they passed over their ten euros each and received their voice tour set in return. They received their instructions for the audio tour and started off. The display was set up in such a way as to walk the visitor through time but the majority of it was related to the Second World War. Jake and Rachel were anxious to get to the underground hideaways. They spent some time looking at the exhibits and tried not to look as though they were rushing through the museum. After what seemed like hours but was only about forty minutes, they reached the opening leading down.

"Don't I look cute?" joked Rachel as she dubiously donned the required bright yellow hard hat. "Although I have to say that I don't think yellow is my color."

Jake pretended to give her a critiquing stare. "Turn." He imperiously motioned for her to rotate. "I have to have the full effect. Well, it definitely clashes with your outfit and your hairstyle is not going to survive the experience, but overall, yes, you are cute."

Rachel blushed and turned to go down the stairs.

"Careful now, these are pretty steep and not very wide. I guess building things to code wasn't all the important when you are trying to save your life!"

"More likely there was no code!"

Jake looked back at the mouth of the tunnel as he made his way down. Again, the corner of his eye caught some movement. He paused and looked around. He saw only the man with the hat from the ferry who turned away as Jake glanced his way. There's an odd one for you, he thought.

Dismissing him and the other tourists from his mind, he gave his attention to the rock around him. The tunnel had been carved out of the limestone bedrock. The walls were jagged and cratered in areas. Electric lights had been strung along the top of the tunnels and provided enough light that he could avoid tripping over the unevenness of the floor. He could smell the damp dirt smell that must simply be part of the atmosphere of the tunnels all the time. It wasn't overpowering, and in fact, he found the air fresher than he was expecting. He now understood the need for the hard hats. The roof in places was quite low and the doorways even lower. He tried to imagine spending every night down in these tunnels with everyone from your town. How crowded they must have been. How the damp earth smell would have been overwhelmed by the smell of sweat and fear. He wondered at the fortitude of the young children who would have played every evening for years down in these tunnels. And he wondered at the display of love, as their parents would have had to try to make things as normal for them as possible.

They moved through the tunnels, entering communal sleeping areas that had bunk beds for 8 or 12 people. Those rooms were far less claustrophobic although were not roomy by any description. They came to the first aid room, the surgical 'suite' and the nursery; all of which would have been used during the Second World War. Some of the tunnels lead on to the next one but some were dead ends, and they had to backtrack. They began to give their attention to the walls.

"The only thing I can think of," said Jake, "is that he would have carved a message into the walls. That is the only place where something could be hidden." He looked up. "Except I guess the roof, but that would be pretty difficult to do."

"I would think that it would have to be relatively easy and if it was a message, short. Otherwise, it would be more likely to be found. Do you think it is in words or would Raphael have used symbols?" asked Rachel.

Jake shrugged. "Your guess is as good as mine. I agree with the short part, but I have no idea what he would have used."

They continued slowly through the tunnels trying to make out some pattern or message carved into the rock. They took their time and often paused as other tourists went past. Jake kept an eye out for the man he had seen before. He was not one of those who passed them.

"This is going to be impossible," Rachel said. She was feeling very discouraged. The walls and ceiling for that matter were entirely pitted and marked. The chiseling of the rock had left marks resembling ripples across the ocean. Only they were less organized. "I can't imagine that he would have just carved something into the rock where just anyone could see it. And if it isn't in plain sight, I can't tell how we will know if he carved it."

"Well, I agree with you that he wouldn't have done it where it would be easily found. If he had, the people who stayed down here in the bombing raids of World War II would have found it. So, let us get off the beaten track."

All along the larger main tunnel, they had seen many tunnels branching off. Some were part of the tour and others were blocked off. Here and there some were left open without any instruction. Jake hunched over a bit and stepped into a narrower tunnel. Rachel looked at the opening and then into the part farther in.

She looked dubious. "I don't know, Jake. That looks pretty small. Surely a Knight wouldn't be able to fit down there. And I'm not sure I want to see if I fit down there."

Jake turned back and held out his hand. "Remember the size of the armor we saw. The Knights weren't as tall or as heavy as we are today. They would have fit more comfortably that us. Take my hand. I'll go first. If it gets so tight that I can't fit, you should still have plenty of room. Besides, this area still has lights strung. If it were too dangerous, they wouldn't want people down here so it wouldn't be lit."

Cautiously she put her hand in his. "I still don't think this is a good idea."

"Nothing ventured, nothing gained." Jake flashed his most winsome smile at her. She did look a little pale.

She hesitantly stepped into the branching tunnel. The roof was grazing the top of her hard hat, and the walls were definitely closer to her. She did still have room between herself and the walls at least. Taking a firm hold of Jake's hand, she took a deep breath. "Okay, let's go."

Jake lead them on slowly. Rachel tried not to think about the tons of rock on top of them and the buildings, roads, cars and people on top of the rock. She tried not to think about a cave-in that would trap them in this tunnel. That if a cave-in happened, they would be entombed forever. There would be no rescue. Silly to think about a cave-in, she chided herself silently. These tunnels survived being bombed again and again. There isn't suddenly going to be a cave-in in any of these tunnels let alone the one you happen to be in. Her internal pep talked helped calm her. She tried to focus more on the walls than on the clenching in her stomach.

As they continued, the tunnel became narrower. Both of them started to have to walk almost sideways. Jake walked looking at one side and her at the other. Rachel was glad that he continued to hold her hand. Jake's shirt began to catch from time to time on the rough outcroppings from the wall. Rachel could feel her heart rate rising. She became much more conscious of the thumping of her heart in her chest. Focusing on the walls became almost impossible for her. Her palms started to sweat. She concentrated on keeping her breathing even and slow. She knew that there wasn't much between her and a full blown panic attack. The wall behind her began to brush against her shoulders. She tried to focus on the wall in front of her.

"I still don't see how we are going to find these. These walls are no better than the other ones and maybe even worse."

Jake sensed she was anxious and squeezed her hand reassuringly. "You are doing great. We are going to have to turn back soon as it is getting pretty tight for me."

"You aren't going to get stuck, are you?" Rachel's voice rose to a high pitch. Visions of Jake being squeezed between the two walls rose in front of her. What would she do? How would she get him out? How would she get help? The panic that she had been trying to keep at bay swept through her.

Suddenly, the lights went out.

Rachel screamed. "What's happened? Why did the lights go out? What is going on? Are you stuck? What are we going to do? I need to get out, get out, out," She couldn't keep herself from babbling. Terror welled up into her throat, all of her fear of being trapped, crushed under piles of rock, surfaced. She could feel the walls pushing in on her chest; she could feel herself start to suffocate. She started to breath more quickly. She knew she was going to die. Tears she was unable to suppress sprang to eyes and ran down her face. She began to sob. "I don't want to die."

"Shhhh, it's okay." She could hear Jake moving and then she felt his arm around her neck. He pulled her head down onto his shoulder. The tunnel was too tight for him to be able to hold her better than that. "Shhhh, focus on my breathing. Match your breathing to mine. Slow it down. You are having a panic attack, nothing more. Darkness is harmless. People know we are down here. Help will come. We aren't stuck, we can easily get out, the roof won't collapse. You aren't going to die. Focus on my breathing. That's it." His voice was steady and firm. She tried to match her breathing to his. She clung to his words as she calmed. She started to feel the warmth radiating from Jake and the solidness of his shoulder under her head. She could feel her heart rate slowly dropping.

"Take slow even breaths. That's right. It's okay. Nothing has changed except the lights went out. We are together, and we know the direction from which we came so we can make our way back." Jack conveniently didn't mention that two or three turns they had made. He wasn't sure he would be able to navigate those in the dark, but she didn't need to know that. He could feel that she was calming.

Slowly Rachel pulled herself back together. She began to feel the pain of the uneven walls pressing into her as she had turned to face Jake despite the narrowness.

"I think I'm okay now." Her voice was shaky. Jake gave her a quick squeeze and released her. She tried to wipe the tears off her face as best she could. Like any five-year-old with no Kleenex, she was reduced to wiping her nose on her shirt sleeve. Panic leaves you with no pride she thought.

Taking a deep breath, she asked, "What do we do now?"
"Well, in most situations, it's best to stay put until the rescue arrives."

"But are they even going to know we are down here?" Her voice quavered despite her attempts to appear calm.

"Oh, I'm sure they keep a pretty close count on tickets sold, people in and people out. They don't want anyone staying down here any more than we want to stay. Besides, we can start backtracking in a minute."

He began to run his fingers along the walls trying to get his bearings. Just before the lights had winked out, he thought he had seen something. He concentrated now on his fingertips.

"Why in a minute? Can't we go now?"

"Just a minute."

"What is it, Jake?"

Jake didn't answer.

"What?"

Rachel could hear the panic starting to rise in her voice again.

"It's okay. Just before the lights went out, I thought I had seen some grooves on the wall which were smoother than others. I have just been sliding my hands along the wall and, well, give me your fingers." He took her hand and gently moved it along the wall. "Can you feel the difference?"

She shook her head forgetting that he couldn't see her. "No."

Jake moved his fingers over the wall again. Yes, there it was, he was sure. "Some of the grooves are definitely smoother than others. Not very many but they seem to be clustered together. Do you have a pen? No, something thicker than that, a marker?"
Rachel squirmed around until she was able to get her arm into her handbag. She pulled out her lipstick. "I have lipstick. "

"Can you get it to me?"

Rachel squirmed enough to be able to transfer the lipstick from one hand to the other. She held it out towards Jake. His hand wrapped around hers and he took the lipstick.

"Excellent."

He opened the tube and wound up the lipstick. Carefully, he found what he thought was the first groove of the series. He traced it with his finger and kept the lipstick beside his finger as he traced. When he got to the end of it, he lifted the lipstick and started on the next one.

Rachel shifted impatiently. She had no idea what he was doing. Curiosity about what he was doing had the beneficial side effect of keeping her anxiety about their situation in check. "Jake…"

"Just a minute, I have to concentrate." He continued to explore the wall, tracing the smooth grooves with the lipstick. Finally, he seemed to get to the end of the pattern. "Now, I just have to get my phone."

There was no way he was going to be able to reach. "Rachel, I need you to reach into my back pocket and get out my phone. Please do not drop it."

He shifted his back towards her as much as he could. Rachel reached over and found the small of his back. The feel of his back muscles moving under his shirt helped to calm her even more. Running her hand down his back, she was able to locate the phone. Carefully, she worked it out of the pocket. Again, they were able to make the transfer. Turning on the flashlight, he was able to highlight the area of the wall that he had marked.

Everything about their situation, including her appreciation for his well muscled behind, was forgotten. Rachel was appalled. "Jake, you have smeared lipstick all over a historical monument. How could you? Why did you do that? Were you trying to lay a trail for people to find us?"

As if on cue, they could hear distant shouting. Rachel forgot her need to be rescued in the horrifying knowledge that if they were rescued from this exact spot, they would have hours of explaining what they had been doing and why they had defaced a world heritage site.

"Come on," she tugged his sleeve urgently. "We need to get out of this spot before they find us here. They can't see this mess you have made." She closed her eyes. "I can't imagine what they would say. What the university would say if they found out?"

"Wait, we need to get photos of this and then we will go meet them up the tunnel. I don't want them knowing about this any more than you do. Chances are no one ever comes down this way, or if they do, they won't care about a few dabs of lipstick. He began to take photos. He took them from several different angles.

She could hear the rescuers getting closer, their voices echoing off the walls. They didn't have much time to get away from the markings.

"Hurry up," Rachel hissed. "They are almost here."

She called out to the rescue party. "We are here, we're fine, no need to rush."

Finally, he was satisfied. Using his phone flashlight for guidance, they started to move in the direction of the rescuers. Rachel wanted to leave the desecration as far behind them as possible. It couldn't possibly be good if they were caught standing beside it.

A profusely sweating security guard was trying to rush up the tunnel to them. Rachel felt a frisson of relief. He looked like he could barely fit in the tunnel as it was, so there was little chance he would be able to fit further along where the lipstick was. His expression was anxious.

"Int tajjeb? You are both okay? You have no injuries?" He looked them over quickly and seeing no blood seemed to relax. "Ahna huma hekk sorry, we are so sorry; we do not know what happened. Suddenly the lights go out, poof! No warning, no nothing. We are still looking for the why. Liema mess a." His radio crackled. He responded and then listened carefully to the static filled reply.

"Finally, it was found that the main circuit breaker had been shut off." As if on cue, the lights turned on. "It must have been a mistake. A young electrician making a mistake or a new worker at the museum who doesn't know to check that all people are out before turning out the lights. Although usually we just turn them out, we don't shut the circuit breaker."

During this monolog, they had been able to get back to the main tunnel.

"Would you like to finish the tour? Please, I will take you."

"No, thank you," said Rachel very emphatically. "You are very kind, but I think I have had enough of being underground for some time."

Rachel was grateful to step out into the sunshine. The heat of the sun felt wonderful after the damp coldness of the tunnels. She fussed a bit with her hair realizing that between the hard hat and her complete loss of control, she must be a bit of a mess. Giving up, she figured it was probably a lost cause at this point.

"Never will I complain about it being too hot again. I have no idea how the Maltese survived all those nights of bombing. I'm not sure I could have spent that much time down there. I think I would have taken my chances on the surface!" She shivered. "I still can't believe you lipsticked the walls." She shook her head.

Jake was laughing. "Think about it, Rachel." He laughed again at the sheer irony of it. "The lights going out have meant that we found what we were looking for. They went out the exact moment we were in the exact spot we needed to be."

Rachel smiled. Seeing him so relaxed enable her to throw off the rest of her anxiety. She looped her arm through his. "So where do you want to have a drink to celebrate?"

9

"Thank you," Jake turned away from the counter. He was picking up the package of photo printouts that he had made from his phone. He and Rachel had tried to make sense of the pictures from his phone and then his laptop, but they had gotten nowhere. Both of them had felt that if they had hard copies to work with, things would go better. As he moved away from the counter, he caught a glimpse of a familiar hat and jacket. Was that the same man that had been at the Museum with them?

"Excuse me, excuse me." Jake tried to rush through the other patrons in the store. He emerged into the brilliant sunshine of the Maltese afternoon. Even with his sunglasses, it took some time for his eyes to adjust. He scanned the road up and down. It was a useless exercise. By this time anyone leaving the store before him could have turned down a side street, popped into another shop or just lost themselves in the dozens of tourists walking along the historic road. Besides, he wasn't even sure if he wasn't just paranoid.

Rachel was sitting at a café across the street.

"Did you..." Jake stopped himself. If he was just paranoid, he didn't want to worry her. Yesterday had been a rough day. After they had left the Museum, they had stopped for a glass of wine and an early dinner. The stress of the day had taken its toll on her. She had left him almost immediately after dinner citing the need for a soak in a bathtub and then an early night. She had developed small lines around her eyes that had testified to her exhaustion. Today, she was looking relaxed and happy again. He didn't want to spoil that by asking her if she had seen anything suspicious.

"Did I what?"

"Oh, nothing. I was just going to ask if you had ordered coffee." Jake scanned the people around them but couldn't see anything or anybody worrisome.

Rachel looked at him oddly. "No, I thought we were going back to the Excelsior to look at the photos. Did you want a coffee?"

"No, no, I had just forgotten, that's all. Let's go." Rachel looked at him carefully, trying to read his expression. Something was off. She couldn't put her finger on what it was, but something was off.

Rachel stood and slung her purse over her shoulder. She casually tucked her hand under his arm to prevent them from getting separated in the crowd. Jake liked the feel of her hand resting on his forearm. It helped to dispel the last of the unsettled feeling. He was sure he was overreacting. He quickened his steps to keep pace with Rachel. They were both anxious to get back to the hotel and see what they had.

Jake spread the photos over the table in his room. They had decided that it was best to look at these inside to prevent the breeze from carrying them away. There were ten photos in all. Jake laughed when he looked at two of them. He had undoubtedly been hurrying. One was a picture of the floor, and the other was a fuzzy depiction of his knees. He tossed those aside.

Rachel tried to sort the photos in order. At first glance, they simply looked red smudges on the wall.

"Jake, where's your phone? I want to make sure that I have these in the order that you took them." She looked at him. "Of course, I am assuming that you took them in some semblance of order."

"I think pretty much kept it from left to right. Given I was a bit rushed at the time so it may not be perfect. I was more worried about getting all of it, so there will likely be some overlap between photos. I am pretty sure I didn't miss any of it. This is, of course, assuming that I found all of the lines that I was supposed to, which hopefully I did."

"I hope so too," said Rachel fervently. Just the thought of heading back down into the tunnels brought sweat to her palms.

Using his phone as the reference, they laid them out in the order he took them. The ones that overlapped they put on top of each other to cover the overlap. Given the limited space Jake had had to work in, he had done a good job of getting the photos in focus.

Jake looked at the final result, and his heart fell. "It just looks like a random set of lines. Maybe I was wrong about it."

Rachel was busy studying the photos. "Do you have any paper and a pencil?"

Retrieving the hotel stationary and pen, he handed them to her. She backed slightly away from the table and started to transcribe the lines onto the paper. She tried to keep the distance between the lines proportional to the photos.

"I think this must be a drawing of some sort. Perhaps a map or building." She carefully checked her work. "Look, Jake, in the third photo, do you think that line there is part of the message? It looks a lot smoother than the rest, but you didn't lipstick it."

Jake picked up the photo in question. "Um, I don't know. Maybe. After looking at these, I'm not so sure any of these are actually different or that it means anything at all."

Rachel added that line to her drawing. They both looked at it. A series of random lines on a page. That's all they could see. Both of them felt the disappointment, but neither wanted to acknowledge it.

They had been so sure that it meant something, that they had been on the right track. Jake collapsed into a chair chiding himself for his foolishness. How could he have ever thought that they would find anything? The whole thing was stupid. Why would they be able to figure things out? Why would they, when no one else had in all these years, discover the treasure? What had he been thinking of, taking this trip?

"Well, I guess I can be grateful that I met you on this trip. At least it wasn't a total loss." He said.

"Huh," Rachel was chewing on the end of the pen and not paying any attention to him. She continued to look at the lines, first connecting them in one way and then in another. The possibilities were endless, but maybe, just maybe, she would find something that would help. Used to spending hours in tedious study, reading page after page of information that often wouldn't have anything to do with her research at all, she wasn't ready to give up.

"What was the next clue again? Something about one is not like the other one."

Jake laughed. "That's Sesame Street." He roused himself and found the journal. He quoted "Where the Grand Masters are honored, see which is not the same."

"Okay, so the Grand Masters are most associated with the Palace and the Co-Cathedral. The Palace would have been the offices and living quarters of the current Grand Master and not really where they were honored. They were invested there but not 'honored' per se. That is much more the role of the Co-Cathedral."

She thought furiously. "But why would Raphael draw a diagram of the cathedral? It's a big place. It is divided into sections, so maybe he was trying to point us. Wait." She paused. "Of course, he isn't trying to show us where or how; he is trying to tell us who!"

Rachel began again on a fresh sheet. She quickly redrew the lines, but this time she drew them so that they were side by side, in some cases they were touching.

"Yes!" Her voice was ripe with satisfaction. "And look, if you add that one line that we weren't sure of, it completes it. We did it."

Jake popped up out of the chair and tried to read it over her shoulder. She was bouncing around so much he had to grab her shoulders to hold them still enough to be able to see. In bringing the lines close together and joining some of them, she had discovered that they were in fact letters. And sure enough, that one line that he had missed, when added became the right side of the letter A.

"ZONDADARI. What is it?"

Rachel turned and smiled at him. "Not what but who? He was one of the Grand Masters. Most of the honor of being a Knight and definitely for being the Grand Master came after death when they were buried in the cathedral. Each of the later Grand Masters have monuments in the cathedral. Many of the Knights do as well, but they are more tombstones on the floor of the cathedral. The next clue must be somewhere in the co-cathedral and must have something to do with this Grand Master."

Jake looked at her in admiration. "Let me say again, the best thing about this trip is that I met you. It would have taken me hours to find out all of that but here you are, and you know it all!"

Rachel blushed. "Oh, you could have learned all of that just by googling his name. The internet makes experts of us all."

"Maybe, but I doubt I would have figured out the name in the first place. And I am still really glad I met you. And decided to tell you about all of this."

Rachel flushed a deeper color. "Oh, well, ah, I am too." She wasn't sure if she was more uncomfortable with his words or with the warm feeling that had swept through her. Either way, now wasn't the time to examine it. With an effort, she pulled herself together. "Come on, why are we still here? We have a place to go and a person to see, even if he has been dead for several hundred years."

"Wait a minute." Jack stacked the photos together and popped them back in the envelope. He opened his closet and unzipped the front pocket of his suitcase. He slid the packet inside and tucked it back in. "Just in case the maid decides to be curious. We don't want anyone figuring out we were the ones that lipsticked a national monument!"

As they retraced their steps back into the city, Rachel told him more about the co- cathedral.

"People get confused about the co-cathedral part of the name. Some people think that it is because there is another St John's Cathedral somewhere else, but if that were the case, every cathedral would be a co-cathedral. Some people think it is because it shared its importance with the Grand Master's palace which also isn't the case. A co-cathedral is called this when there are two cathedrals in an area which can both serve as the bishop's seat. In the case of this Cathedral, St John's was the cathedral of the Order and the bishop's seat until the Order was expelled. After that time, the cathedral in Mdina gained in importance and became the bishop's seat. In the early 1800's, the archbishop of Malta allowed St John's to become an alternate of the cathedral in Mdina. So it became a co-cathedral. It is quite a stunning place. I have always wanted to visit. I have an entire book on it. I have looked at those pictures over and over.

Jake lifted a hand. "Question. What's a bishop's seat? Why is it so special?"

"The bishop's seat is literally the seat that he sits in. As you might imagine, it isn't simply a wooden chair. But more importantly, it represents the bishop's teaching authority."

"But doesn't that belong to the Pope? I admit to not knowing much about church. My mom used to make me go, but I spent most of my time making faces at the girls. If I made them laugh, they would get in trouble. Of course, come to think of it, so would I." He smiled at the memory of his mother. "Anyway, by the time I was eight or nine she had had enough of trying to keep me still and behaving. She left me with Dad and went alone." At the time, Jake had been ecstatic that she had left him at home. Sunday mornings had become times when he and his dad would go hiking or fishing. Now he regretted that he hadn't been mature enough to see how much it would have meant to his mother for him to go with her. Her faith had been an important part of who she had been. He had seen only the boredom of sitting still.

"Are you okay? Jake? I think I've lost you." Rachel laid her hand on his arm. Without intending to, Jake took her hand in his. It felt right, so he kept a hold of it.

"Sorry, I'm fine. I get lost sometimes thinking about my mom. Anyway, tell me more about the co-cathedral."

They had entered the city while they had been talking and were now standing in the square outside of the church. It stood as an imposing building only because of its size. From where they were standing, it was simply a big, old, gray building with some windows. While they were stained glass, it was hard to see that from the square. Even the belfry and steeple were relatively nondescript. It was certainly not something that Jake would have expected given the stories of the Knights and their riches.

"I admit it looks very plain on the outside. But the interior is very elaborate. Initially, it wasn't nearly as ornate as it is now. One of the Grand Masters decided that it needed to be upgraded to be closer to the opulence of the cathedrals in Rome. It was made over at that time. Then the Grand Masters' all started to build tombs for themselves. These tombs became more and more elaborate. Some of the Grand Masters' starting building their tombs not long after they were elected. Although, in their defense, many of them didn't serve as Grand Master for more than three or four years before they ended up dying."

They joined the queue for entrance into the cathedral. As they entered, Rachel accepted the shawl given to her at the door and draped it around her shoulders. As with many churches, she had forgotten that there was a requirement for covering her shoulders. Thankfully her shorts were long enough that they didn't make her take one of the skirts to put on.

Despite the dozens of people in the cathedral, there was a respectful hush as they made their way in. Having looked at photos of the interior before, Rachel knew what to expect. Despite this, the reality was far more than she had imagined. Both of them looked around the cathedral in awe. Every square inch of the place seemed to be covered in marble or gold. Jake wasn't sure where to look first. Rachel took his arm.

"Let's just play tourist for a bit before we look for the monument. I know both of us are anxious to find the next clue, but this is so beautiful, let's just enjoy for a while. I want to soak it in. I will give you a tour."

Jake could only nod his agreement still taking in his surroundings. He found it overwhelming and difficult to focus on any one thing.

Rachel pulled his arm to get his attention. He focused on her face.

Keeping her voice low, Rachel said, "Let's start with the floor. These are the tombstones of many of the Knights who were held in high esteem by the Order as well as some of the Grand Masters. They are so beautiful."

Each tombstone was a complex mosaic of beautiful marble. Together, they incorporated multiple colors turning the floor into a vast collection of green, red, blue, white and black. Each monument fit neatly against the one beside it. Rows of chairs sat in the center of the cathedral facing the altar covering some of the more central monuments.

"The tombstones will have the name of the Knight as well as some description of his exploits or dedication to the Order. You can see if you look carefully at them, that there are themes that are repeated in most of them." She pointed out the skeleton in the two they were currently standing on.

"Skeletons were seen as representing the beginning of life on earth as well as the beginning of life eternal. They weren't perceived as gross or scary as they tend to be looked at now. And look at the angels." She pointed out several in the stones around them. "See how they are holding either trumpets or wreaths? These were meant to signify victory. The wreaths depicted laurel wreaths which were often given to victors of competitions. "

Rachel fell silent. She absorbed the sense of history around her, trying to imagine what life would have been like during the time these Knights lived. She could envision the Knights gathering for a service, resplendent in their robes. She could see them each with their sword at their side clanking as they stood or knelt. She smiled. Kneeling and then getting up without catching their swords in their robes and toppling over must have been a bit of a learning curve for the new Knights. Then she wondered if they had been allowed to wear their swords in the church. She hadn't come across anything one way or the other in her research. She tucked that question into her memory for future investigation.

Jake, despite the splendor around them, watched Rachel's face. Her face had relaxed, and her eyes had gone softer. He could tell she was thinking about how it had been. She was reliving history. He was grateful that he had met her and even more so that they had been able to get past the awkward beginning. He knew that she was becoming more important to him than simply as a co-treasure hunter. He looked forward every morning to seeing her smile. He found himself working to trigger that smile throughout the day. He enjoyed the 'dissertations' as he called them about the Knights. She was so intelligent and yet made everything so clear. He loved her sense of humor. He chuckled to himself. He probably loved her sense of humor because she thought his jokes were funny. Or she was at least polite enough to laugh at them. When he was with her, he could feel her love of life radiate from her. He felt a pull inside, a recognition of how important she was becoming to him. He wasn't sure quite what to do with that knowledge yet. Without thinking he reached up and tucked a piece of her hair behind her ear. She came back to the present with a start.

"What?" Rachel felt off balance. His touch had startled her out of her reverie. She was taken aback by the look in his eyes. "Oh, sorry." She covered her confusion by unfolding the map of the cathedral and then refolding it. "I got lost thinking about the past." When she looked at him again, it was the same old Jake.

Jake smiled. "Yes, I have noticed that that happens to you. I like it."

Rachel flushed. "Anyway, moving on, let's go up to the sanctuary. Today, people use the word 'sanctuary' to mean the entire gathering place in a church. Basically where the congregation sits. In these days, the sanctuary was the altar. There is the marble statue depicting the baptism of Christ by John the Baptist up at the front. That area has a unique name, but I can't remember what it is. At one point there was a painting of the baptism there, but it was removed and replaced by the statute. And I do have to say; it is pretty impressive."

As they approached the altar, Rachel continued her tour commentary. "If you look closely, you can see in the middle of the altar, a frieze of the Last Supper. When they redid the cathedral, they tended to do it in the Baroque fashion, and the altar is the ultimate example of that."

Jake leaned closer to her ear. "What's a frieze?"

"Oh, sorry. It's just a fancy word for a horizontal carving that is longer than it is high."

Together they gazed around the altar, taking in the magnificent pipes of the pipe organ, the ornate silver lamps, and the incredible candlestick holders.

"How many pipes do you think this organ has?" he asked.

Rachel shook her head.

"I have no idea. That isn't my area of expertise. But speaking of expertise, look up at the ceiling."

Jake craned his neck upwards and immediately wished that everyone would go away so he could lie on his back on the floor to appreciate the ceiling.

"This looks like the Sistine Chapel." He said.

"Yes," Rachel replied. "It is painted very much like the Sistine Chapel. Of course, St John is the patron saint of the Order. The ceiling depicts his life from the moment Zachary was told he would be born to the moment he was beheaded. Unlike the Sistine Chapel, it doesn't contain the secular imagery that Michelangelo worked into his paintings. But it is spectacular. It was painted by one of the members of the Order, I think his name was Preti but don't quote me on it."

Jake shook his head. "I don't know how you remember any of this stuff. History for me was simply something to learn long enough to write the exam and then dump out of my memory."

They stood and enjoyed the ceiling until a group of Japanese tourists and their flag holding tour guide started to crowd around them on their own tour through the cathedral.

"Time to move on," Jake said.

They moved to the side of the church where different factions of the Order had their individual small chapels. Jake had already learned that because of the different languages within the group, the Knights had been divided up based on from where they had come. They lived with those who had come from the same region.

Jake recognized the large monuments in each chapel as being the monuments to the Grand Masters.

"Wow, these are pretty impressive. I guess humility wasn't a virtue that was necessary for a Grand Master!"

Rachel laughed quietly. "Well, if you were to go and look at Jean de

La Vallette's tomb, you would find that it is much less ornate and is placed in a much less lavish part of the cathedral. Typical of human nature, as the Order developed over time, ego started to play a bigger role. Like all organizations, I suspect that they weren't all like that. Come on; let's find Zondadari's monument."

They moved from chapel to chapel stopping the check to names on the monuments. Jake commented to Rachel that it would have been much easier if they had had a map which labeled all the monuments. But then, most people weren't looking for a specific one. Finally, they found Zondadari's. Compared to some of the others, it wasn't overly elaborate but still had enough carving and different pieces to it that they knew that this wasn't going to be an easy task.

"Okay, so the clue is 'Where the Grand Masters are honored, see which is not the same.' The tunnels pointed us to Zondadari and now what?" Rachel asked.

"Well, let's look at what isn't the same. You have two cherubs which are in different positions; you have what I presume is a depiction of the Grand Master himself reclining on the coffin but only one of him. At the top, there are lots of different spears pointing upwards. And a whole bunch of other carvings here and there." Jake fell silent. "What if this is like Sesame Street?"

Rachel looked at him like he had lost his mind.

"Bear with me. What if it is like what you said earlier, you know, the 'which one of these is not like the others' jingle?"

"Well, if that is the case, then there would have to be more than one thing which is the same so that one of them could be different. Isn't that how it worked?"

"Correct. And the multiples would have to be exactly the same except for the one that is what we want." They turned back to examine the monument.

"Okay, there are multiple spears, but I have to say that they all look the same to me. There are multiple cherubs if you include the ones at the top, but two out of the four are different. It looks like there are multiple crests but again, none of them are exactly the same. I hate to say it, but this is like looking for a needle in a haystack."

"Think Jake; this monument would have been here for years before all of this happened. Zondadari died in 1722. The French didn't come until the beginning of the 1800's. Raphael wouldn't have been able to change a big part of the monument. So either by some strange coincidence, this monument had exactly what he needed to fit the clue, or he was able to modify something without drawing attention to it, without anyone noticing."

They returned to looking at it.

"There, what's that?" Rachel's voice rose in excitement. "Down at the bottom, there are four panels of rose marble, those are all the same. But the one on this end, it looks like something is a bit different. "

Jake looked where she was pointing. Too late, he thought about the possibility that someone was following them. He had been so overwhelmed by the cathedral that he had totally forgotten to be on the look out for that odd man in the hat and jacket. Now, if he had been following them, they had not only led him directly to the correct monument but Rachel was currently pointing out the exact clue. Jake grabbed her arm to lower it. She looked up at him oddly.

"No point in pointing it out to everyone. People might start asking questions." As an excuse, it was pretty lame, and Rachel's expression clearly showed that she agreed with that assessment. Jake moved on hoping to smooth it over.

"Let's look at that more closely." Jake took out his phone and started to take a few photos of the monument. Just in case someone was watching, he started by taking some of the whole thing and then close-ups of different parts of it. Rachel continued to watch him. Finally, he took photos of the bottom marble panels.

Rachel crowded behind his shoulder as he enlarged the photo on his screen.

"There's something there. And it doesn't look like it was carved by a master carver either." Rachel's voice rang with excitement. Several people around them looked over in response to her voice. "Oops. I guess I was a bit loud. Let's see it." She said more quietly.

Jake turned his phone off. "Come on, I'm starving and could do with a drink. Let's get out of here now. We can always come back another time if we need to."

Rachel became aware of her own empty stomach. They had had a late breakfast while waiting for the photos to be printed but they had skipped lunch. She glanced at her watch.

"Jake, it's 4:30 pm. We've been here for almost 4 hours!" She couldn't believe it.

"Well, it was worth every minute of it. Let's go find a drink and some dinner."

10

Jake and Rachel could hardly keep themselves from looking at the photos. But they agreed that they would do better if they had something to eat first. They had returned to the hotel to freshen up a bit before going for dinner. Rachel found Jake waiting for her in the hotel lobby. As she crossed the room, she gave a small sigh of relief. He had changed into dress pants with a light sports coat. That meant she wasn't overdressed. Rachel had felt like a teen on her first date while changing. She had tried on at least three different outfits trying to figure out which was most appropriate. Finally, she decided that she was going to wear what she felt nice in and not think about what 'statement' it might make. She had finally selected a light sheath dress and had broken out her pumps to go with it. In retrospect, she wasn't even sure why she had packed them. Why she had thought she would need heels on this trip was a mystery to her, although ironically, it appeared that she did need them. Well, 'need' might not be the correct term.

He looked her up and down and gave an appreciative whistle.

"Don't we both clean up well? I like your shoes, they do great things for your legs, but are you sure you can walk in those?"

She laughed. "All female teenagers, or at least the girly girls, spend hours practicing walking in heels so to be able to impress their dates. Besides," she did a quick cha-cha-cha, "if I can dance in them, I can walk in them."

"All right then. That settled, let's go for dinner." Jake tucked her hand into the crook of his arm and escorted her across the lobby. Outside was a sleek Mercedes sedan with the door held open by one of the bellman.

"I thought we were walking?" Rachel was confused.

"Oh, we will, but I thought it would be fun to use the hotel's car service to get us to the top of the hill."

Rachel slid into the back seat and Jake joined her.

"The front gate of Valletta."

"Very good, sir."

Rachel giggled a bit as the driver headed out the driveway.

"My goodness, I have never had a chauffeur on a date before." Realizing what she had said, she started to blush. She could feel the heat rising in her cheeks. "I mean, not that this is a date or anything but I mean I've never…" she trailed off.

Before she could think about it, she blurted out the question.

"I don't even know if you have a girlfriend."

Jake laughed. "Nope, no girlfriend, unless you count the furry one with four legs and a tail also known as my cat. Although, come to think of it, she can be quite possessive. I'm okay with it being a date." Rachel had no response to that.

He helped her out of the car after arriving at the front gate.

Once again he took her hand as they walked into the city. "I spoke with the concierge, and they recommended that we try the King's Own. It is a bar/restaurant that has an excellent reputation. The King's Own is a band that has been in existence for some time apparently. The concierge mentioned that they were the first band to play the national anthem of Malta when they achieved independence. I thought that you might appreciate that little bit of history."

They made their way down the Rue Republic. The street was lit up with bright signs and strings of light. Pools of light streamed through the open doors of the many restaurants and bars. The muted hum of voices was broken by the clink of crystal glasses raised in a toast and punctuated by the sounds of laughter. Tables and chairs had appeared along the road where there had been none during the day. They signaled the opening of a restaurant closed during regular business hours. The temperature was perfect, and the air was still. Both of them were silent as they walked. They simply absorbed the atmosphere around them and enjoyed each others company.

"Here we are." Jake broke the silence. He stepped back to allow Rachel to enter first. Fantastic smells of delicious sauces and a multitude of spices were thick in the air. Jake gave an appreciative sniff. "Well, if their food is anything like it smells, this place will be great."

The hostess smiled and greeted them. "Yes, you will find that the food is even better than it smells. For two?"

"Yes, please."

She led them back into the restaurant. It was almost full and there was little room between the tables. As they made their way back to their table, both Jake and Rachel unobtrusively tried to look at the food on other patrons' plates.

The hostess placed the menus on the table in front of them.

"Diana will be your server today. The specials are a roasted rabbit ravioli in a light creamy sauce, and grill turbot served on a bed of barley pilaf with steamed broccolini. Enjoy."

Rachel didn't even open her menu. "After looking at all the other food people were eating as we came in, I thought this was going to be a difficult choice. Luckily, I don't need to open the menu. I have to have rabbit at least once while I am here. It is the national dish."

"Sounds good to me. Do you prefer red or white wine?"

"Red is my preference, if you don't mind."

Diana came to their table and greeted them. She brought water and the usual bread basket. "Can I get you something else to drink or do you need a few minutes?"

Rachel replied. "I am so hungry I would like to order my food if that is okay. Jake, are you all right with that?"

"Works for me." As Rachel ordered her meal, Jake perused the wine list and selected a merlot from Chile. "It is full-bodied enough to have good flavor but shouldn't overpower the rabbit. Which," he smiled at Diana, "I will also have."

"Excellent choices. I'll put those orders in for you so that you don't have to wait long, and I will be back with your wine."

Rachel plucked a piece of warm fresh bread from the basket and sighed with delight.

"So, Jake," she contemplated the butter while thinking about the added calories. Shrugging she started to butter the bread. Tonight was not a night she was going to stress about calories. "Tell me a bit about yourself. I don't know that much beyond the fact that you have an ancestor who was a Knight and that your father was a bloodthirsty young boy! What about your mom? Do you have brothers or sisters?"

Jake sighed and retrieved his own piece of bread. They paused as the wine appeared, was opened with all the usual fuss and poured.

Jake tasted it, nodded at the waitress that it was good and she filled their glasses.

"No brothers or sisters. It was always just the three of us. Now it is just my dad and me. My mom died suddenly about eight months ago. She was always the one that had held the family together. She made sure that holidays were special and that we kept in touch. If I was too busy to call or email, she would find ways to let me know that it had been too long since I had been in contact. She somehow managed to make you feel good about everything, even if it wasn't something particularly good." Jake paused and sifted through his memories. "I still remember when I was chosen last for a drama team in elementary school. I was really upset. I was used to being either captain of a sports team or picked fairly high up the list. Drama wasn't my strong suit, so it isn't surprising that they didn't want me on their team. I didn't care about the project, but boy, did it sting my pride being the last one picked. Rather than trying to make me feel better about being picked last, my mom sat me down and pointed out that being picked last happened to other kids all the time. That my own experience would help me understand what they felt like when they were picked last. She also pointed out that by being the last one that time, I had kept some other kid from feeling upset. Somehow that made me feel better about things at the time. I know that after that whenever I picked a kid last, I made sure that he knew that it wasn't because I didn't want him on the team. I went out of my way to try to make sure that he wouldn't feel bad about being the last one. I don't know if it made them feel better or even made sense to them, but I felt better about it."

He took a drink of water to allow the lump that had developed in his throat with recounting that memory to dissolve.

"It sounds as if she was very special. You must miss her a lot."

"I do. I hadn't realized was how much she was keeping my dad on track. She was looking after him more than I knew. Since she died, he has struggled. They had a pretty traditional marriage with him working and her doing the cooking and cleaning. There has been a learning curve for him. It took a while for him to realize that if clean underwear was going to show up in the drawer, he had to wash it and put it there. I talked him into hiring a housekeeper pretty soon after Mom died, but he refuses to hire someone to cook or even to get a meal service that would bring him meals. He insists that he is learning to cook for himself. But every time I see him he is a bit thinner, and there never seems to be much in the fridge except beer. I have started to try to take him out for dinner more often and have given him gift certificates to restaurants close to the house. Other than that, I don't know what to do to help. He always says he is fine, but I don't know." Jake felt his eyes mist over. He blinked rapidly and looked off over the ocean. "It hurts to see him hurt."

Rachel reached over and gave his hand a squeeze. "Your parents must have loved each other very much. These days that isn't as common as I'd like to think. You are very lucky to have had them. I am sure that your dad will continue to try to find his way. I can see that the first year without someone would be very tough. Especially when they meant that much to you. "

Jake turned his hand over and laced his fingers between hers. "And what about you? Happy family? Parents still together? Still alive? Siblings?"

The food arrived before she could reply, and they broke apart. The next few minutes were devoted to savoring the complex flavors of their meals.

"You were right. This wine is perfect." She sighed with delight at the mix of flavours from the ravioli and the wine. "This is wonderful. But, I owe you my family history. We are simply one big happy family. My parents got together in high school and have been together ever since. I have two brothers and three sisters, believe it or not. My brothers and one sister are all working away on their careers while my other sisters are busy making my parents happy by providing them with grandchildren. So far, there are six grandchildren, all under the age of nine. Family get-togethers are loud and busy. But we all get along well together most of the time. Certainly, if any one of us is in trouble, the rest of the family will rally around pretty quickly whether you want them to or not. Needless to say, I haven't said very much to them about the professor as I am pretty sure my brothers would fly to England and show up in his office demanding him to be nicer to me."

"Why did you decide to get a Ph.D. in history? That is a long slog to get through and with all due respect to your hard work, there can't be very many places you can use that."

Rachel smiled ruefully. "That's exactly what Tim, my eldest brother said when I was accepted into the program. He's a doctor. So he is very practical and science oriented. He doesn't understand why anyone would do anything related to an arts degree. I love history. I think that we fail to understand or appreciate the meaning of history and what it can tell us about ourselves. Most history is taught as a long list of events and dates. That is about as exciting as reading an old printed dictionary. There is a certain amount of truth to the statement that history repeats itself. I want to show people how things cycle over time. How similar we have been over the years and even over cultures and geography. That, I think is the real value of history. I believe we should be teaching that to children from the beginning. Which means, of course, I will likely end up a teacher. Ideally, at some point, I'd like to be a teacher's teacher and help educators learn to teach history in a meaningful way.

Her hand hovered over the bread basket as she tried to decide if she wanted another piece. That wasn't quite accurate. She knew she wanted another piece, just as she knew that she didn't need it. Feeling very virtuous, she decided against it.

"My mum and dad have always been very supportive of all of us in what we have wanted to do. Tim's a cardiologist, Mike's a paediatrician, and Lisa is a financial something or other. Analyst, planner, I can't figure out exactly what she does. My other two sisters both have degrees but then decided to stay home to raise their kids. They all live within an hour's drive of Mum and Dad. Mum and Dad still live in the house where we all grew up. I was always a bit of a misfit. My mother used to despair that I was too dreamy and easily distracted. I was forever making up backstories for my dolls; where did they come from, what were their families like, that kind of thing. I would spend hours on my history homework but Mum would have to practically stand over me to get me to do my math and science homework." She laughed. "I even liked English because I could find out the history behind where words came from. I'm probably one of the few people in the world who are sad that we don't learn Latin anymore. I know, people think I'm crazy." She put her elbows on the table and her chin in her hands. "What about you?

"Well, I think my career chose me rather than the opposite. I was forever picking up injured animals and bringing them home. Neighbors started bringing me birds that had fallen from nests or had broken wings. They brought kittens they found left at the side of the road or orphaned raccoons. We lived out in the country, and there wasn't an animal rescue or SPCA around to look after them, so I ended up doing it." Jake smiled at the memory. "One day someone showed up with two baby skunks that had been orphaned. Their mother had been hit by a car. My mother was horrified when she found out I had two skunks in a box in my room. That was the day Mom made my dad build a small house in the backyard for all the animals. She was adamant that there would be no skunks in the house, so I spent the first few days sleeping in the garage with them to make sure they got fed regularly. Baby skunks don't develop their scent sacks until they are older but that didn't matter. There was no way she was letting them inside. People ask me why I didn't become a doctor instead of a vet. I never could deal with a person getting injured. I used to pass out anytime someone was bleeding but bring me a raccoon baby that was abandoned or injured, and I would spend hours fixing them, feeding them and rehabilitating them. Luckily most of the demand for animal care was in the summer when I was on holidays. Unlike most kids, I never wanted to go to Disneyland or anything like that. When my parents asked me what I wanted to do for holidays, it was always something like expanding the animal house or building a new enclosure." Jake looked thoughtful. "Now, I realize that they gave up their own holiday time to do that for me. Only once that I can remember did they asked my grandparents to stay with me for a week. They took off on their own for that week." He reflected on what they had given him over the years. "I had great parents."

Two hours later they were sitting, laughing at some silly story Jake had told about one of his puppy patients who kept getting into the same trouble over and over and needed the same treatment again and again.

Rachel toyed with her wine glass. "This was lovely, thank you, Jake. It was wonderful just to sit and enjoy a great meal with a good friend. And I do have to say, the food was amazing."

Jake warmed at the thought that she felt he was a good friend. He raised his glass.

"To fantastic food and good friends." They both finished off their wine.

"Well, let's head back and take a look at what we found today." Rachel pushed back her chair and put her napkin on her placemat. "Before we go, I have to find the little girls room."

"No worries, I'll deal with the bill and then we can head out."

Jake looked around the room for Diana. He signaled to her to bring the bill. As he turned back around, he caught a flash of that same jacket and hat passing the doorway that he had seen earlier. A chill ran through him. Was it really the same?

"I'll be right back." Jake rushed past a surprised Diana and hurried to the front door. He looked left and right trying to see if he could see the jacket. The street was jammed with people. Looking right was a lost cause as the road ran uphill and the crush of people meant he couldn't see anything beyond about six feet. Looking downhill, he could easily make out individuals. He scanned the crowd but was unable to see the jacket. Either the wearer had disappeared, or he was overreacting and making things up.

He returned to the table and settled the bill. By that time, Rachel was back.

"Ready to go?"

Again, as they reached the door, Jake tucked Rachel's hand in his arm.

"I wouldn't want you to trip in those shoes." He smiled at her. "Are you in a hurry to get back or do you want to walk a bit, assuming your feet aren't killing you yet?"

"It's such a great night, let's walk. Besides, after that fantastic ravioli and the dessert I didn't need, I could do with a bit of exercise."

They started to make their way down the street. They soon found that it was hard to make any headway without weaving all over the street to avoid groups of people standing and chatting, or eating gelato or simply trying to decide where they were going. Jake continued to scan the crowd, trying to do it without Rachel noticing. He couldn't see anything out of the ordinary.

Rachel gave his arm a tug. "Let's go this way. It's quieter, and I think it leads down to the waterfront. We can walk around to our hotel that way."

They turned off the main road onto one of the side streets. Fairy lights twinkled from strings above them, crisscrossing the road.

Rachel stumbled, and Jake grabbed her arm to keep her from going down.

"Careful there."

She gave a rueful chuckle. "Okay, I admit I should have worn more sensible shoes. It's the cobblestones which make heels difficult. But, that's okay. I'm enjoying myself too much to worry about it."

They continued on and chatted about this and that as people getting to know one another do. Suddenly, Jake heard a funny fuut sound, followed almost immediately by a sting on his cheek.

"Ouch." He put his hand put to his cheek. To his surprise it was sticky. Rachel looked at his fingers.

"You're bleeding. How can you be bleeding?"

He heard another fuut and saw the brick in front of them explode into small chips.

His heart started pounding; he couldn't believe what his eyes and head were telling him. He pulled Rachel around the corner into the next street.

"What..."

"Shhhh. I think someone is shooting at us. I think my cheek is bleeding from the stone chips that came from the wall when the bullet hit it."

Rachel stared at him unable to comprehend what he had said.

"Shooting at us?" Rachel laughed. "Okay, I think all this mystery is making you paranoid."

Another fuut. Brick exploded showering Rachel's shoulder with debris. Jake could only be grateful that the shooter either wasn't very good or didn't have a clear view of them.

Rachel looked at the dirt on her dress in disbelief. "What? Shooting? Why would anyone shoot at us? Who are they? They can have my purse..." Her voice was getting louder and higher with each question. Her pupils were dilated and she was starting to shake.

Jake shook his head, "I don't know what's going on, but I don't think it is simply a mugging. We need to get out of here. Can you run?"
She stared at him, still in a state of denial. Jake didn't wait for an answer.

"Come on," Jake grabbed her hand and started to run down the street just as another fuut sounded behind them. "Run."

As the shooter clearly knew where they were, there wasn't any point in being quiet. They ran to the corner and down the next block and around another corner. Halfway down the lane, Rachel slipped and went down. Jake unceremoniously hauled her to her feet. "Are you okay?"

"Just skinned my knee, that's all. These stupid shoes. I can run better in bare feet." She matter-of-factly reached down and took off her shoes. Jake knew that her sense of calm would be short lived. She was still in shock and not comprehending what was happening.

"Come on."

They started running again. This time Rachel was able to move more quickly. They were also able to be quieter without the clatter of her heels. Jake began to hope that whoever was behind them would not be able to follow. They ran blindly taking corners at random. Finally, Rachel pulled up.

"I have to stop." She was panting heavily. "I need a breather."

Jake pulled her into a small courtyard. "Okay, try to be quiet and let's see if we can hear anything."

He realized that with all of their random running, they had managed to run into an area of the city which was not well lit. A flickering light over a doorway was all that lit the street. He wasn't sure if this was good or bad. On the one hand, it made it harder for them to be found but on the other, it made it more difficult for him to see anyone following them.

Her calm broke.

"Jake", Rachel was clutching at his shirt front. "What's happening? Why is this happening? What are we going to do?"

Jake pulled her in towards him smothering her voice against his chest. The purpose of the embrace was twofold. First, to quiet her and second, to reassure her. She was obviously terrified and despite her willingness to follow his lead when they ran, she hadn't made the link between their treasure hunt and the shooter.

"Shhhh. It's okay." Jake rubbed his hands over her back, trying to sooth her. "Obviously someone doesn't want us looking for this treasure. I'm sure they mean us no real harm and are just trying to scare us."

He jumped as Rachel let out a strangled scream. He was glad he still had her pressed against his chest. If not, the scream would have clearly advertised where they were.

"Something just went around my legs." Panic coloured her words. She stood absolutely still. "Jake, what is it? Is it something bad?"

"Meow."

Jake choked back a laugh. The 'something' was one of the many street cats that prowled Valletta at night. "Hush, stop meowing." The cat continued to wind between their legs and meow piteously. Obviously, it was hoping that they would give it food.

Jake set Rachel away from him. "It's just a cat. It's okay." Rachel stared at the stray.

"Shhhh, be quiet cat." Jake bent down to pat it hoping a bit of affection would silence it. But to no avail.

He stood and looked at Rachel. While she was still pale, she was a bit more in control of herself.

"Can you run or at least walk again, Rachel? I think we have lost him, but I want to get out of here before he finds us or hears this silly cat."

Her voice was still shaky and Jake could see the effort it took to pull herself back together. "Yes, I can walk. I can run if I have to."

He linked his fingers through hers. Rachel felt the warmth and the strength of his hand in hers. She tried to focus on that. Jake would protect her, she knew that. She just couldn't believe that they were in danger. Her breath started to quicken again as a wave of panic swept through her. She turned her thoughts back to Jake's hand. As she calmed down again, she tried to turn off the thoughts of what was happening and concentrate on walking without tripping.

They started down the hill. While Jake didn't have any idea where they were exactly in the city, he knew that they would hit the harbor and the ring road if they kept walking downhill. As they had come from uphill, he didn't want to run the risk of passing their attacker on their way back to the main road. Once they got to it, it would have been safer but all things considered, he thought this was a better choice. He thought about what to do when they reached the road. He had no idea who was shooting at them or why they were being chased. He could only assume that whoever it was had been following them for a while. He began to think that his paranoia about the man in the jacket and hat might not have been paranoia after all. If he had been following them, then he likely knew where they were staying. Jake thought it through. If that was the care, Jake figured that after the two of them had escaped, the shooter would have headed back to the hotel. If he were serious about trying to do them harm, then it would be easiest to ambush them on their way into the hotel. At least, that it was what he would do if he had been the shooter. Walking back was not going to be an option. It left them too vulnerable to another attack as they got closer to the hotel. They had to find a taxi.

They ended up on the ring road not far from Fort St Elmo. Fortunately, there were a number of restaurants in the area, and several taxis were parked nearby hoping for fares. Jake and Rachel gratefully crawled into one.

"Hotel Grand Excelsior, please."

Jake kept an eye out for anything out of the ordinary as they turned into the hotel driveway. It was hard to tell if anything was amiss given that the parking lot at the top of the hill was always at least half full. He wasn't able to see anyone hanging around aimlessly. There was one couple who were on their way back from dinner and obviously very much wanted the privacy of their own room. Jack could see a dark sedan parked down in the circle at the hotel entrance. The tinted windows prevented him from seeing into the car. As they got closer, he could see that it was not a hotel car. He was relieved when the cabbie pulled up right in front of the doors.

"Rachel, I want you to get out my side rather than having to walk around the car. Just in case someone is waiting for us."

"Good evening sir, madam." The doorman opened the door with a flourish. As Rachel and Jake stepped out, he momentarily lost his implacable look.

"Mon Dieu, Qu'est il passe?"

Jake suddenly realized that he would still have blood on his face from the cut. When he turned to look at Rachel, she was limping through the doors leaving little marks of blood behind with each step. Her dress was dirty and her hair which had been sleek and shiny, was now windblown. Both of them had sweat stains from their running.

"Ah, nothing to worry about." Jake pressed a bill into the doorman's hand. "My friend had an encounter with a pickpocket, and we gave chase. We won."

"Would you like me to notify the police?"

Jake almost smiled at the thought of having to explain their situation to the police. "No, no, that's okay. We were able to get her purse back so no harm done."

The doorman looked dubious. "But…"

"Really its fine." Jake caught up with Rachel as she made her way blindly towards the elevators.

Rachel was coming to the end of her coping. She didn't understand what had happened, or perhaps more accurately why it had happened. All she knew at this point was that her feet were painful, her dress was sticking to her, and the adrenaline which had kept her going was quickly draining from her.

Jake could see she was fading quickly. He took her elbow and guided her as fast as she could manage to his room. He sat her on the edge of the second bed.

"Okay, let's take a look at those feet." Jake held each one up. His stomach quivered at the thought of how much pain she must have been having while running on them. Both of them were cut and bleeding in several places. He could see where bruises were going to form overnight.

"I hope your tetanus shot is up to date."

Rachel giggled. Jake looked at her. The giggle grew until she was laughing uncontrollably. "Tetanus shot, shot, shooting…"

Her laugh was tinged with a bit of hysteria. Jake watched her with concern. She fell backwards on the bed shaking with laughter. He wasn't sure if it was better to let her laugh it out or if he should try and stop her. Opting for the easier choice, he decided to continue to clean her feet.

Gently he guided her around on the bed to lie with her legs stretched out. Running the water to fill the sink, he tucked a folded towel under feet. Very gently with a soapy washcloth he slowly washed each foot. As he worked, the laugh dwindled to giggles and then these too, died away. When her feet were clean, he gently inspected them to be sure that there were no bits of stone or even glass in any of the lacerations. When he was satisfied, he covered the cuts with antibiotic ointment. He put Band-Aids over the worst ones. Finished, he looked up to see that Rachel had fallen fast asleep. He gazed at her thinking how beautiful her face was in repose. His heart swelled at how she had reacted tonight. Once she had understood their situation, she hadn't asked unnecessary questions; she hadn't balked at any instructions. She had even run without complaining once about the pain she must have been having. Carefully, he took the blanket from his bed and spread it on top of her.

He bent over and gave her a light kiss on the forehead. "Sleep well, Rachel. You have more than earned it."

11

Rachel stretched and yawned. She debated going back to sleep but the necessity of a visit to the bathroom made that an unlikely choice. She rolled over enjoying the warmth of the bed. She sniffed. She could smell coffee, and that didn't seem right. She was wearing her dress and that didn't seem right. She opened her eyes. She wasn't in her room. Suddenly the events of the last night came back to her in a rush. She sat up immediately. Jake was sitting in an easy chair across the room from her. He had obviously been up for a while as he was freshly showered and dressed. Sitting on the table was a coffee carafe, an extra cup and some fruit and pastries.

"Good morning, Sleeping Beauty."

"What time is it?"

"It's about ten o'clock. But don't worry, you needed the sleep. I thought you deserved at least breakfast in the room, if not in bed. I know you like croissants."

Rachel couldn't believe it was so late. She popped up onto her feet and promptly sat back down on the bed.

Jake winced on her behalf. "Your feet must be really sore. There is some ibuprofen on the bathroom counter for you to take if you want. It will help reduce the pain."

She brushed her hair out of her eyes and suddenly realized that she must look awful. She had worn makeup last night for their dinner and her hair, she could only imagine what her hair looked like. Excusing herself, she grimly stood on her tender feet and hobbled to the bathroom to try to repair what damage she could. The harsh light of the bathroom did nothing to soften the impact of her image. She despaired about what Jake must think of her. Her mascara had bled into dark circles and smudges below her eyes and her hair looked like a rat's nest. She ran a sink full of hot water and scrubbed as much of the damage off her face as she could. She used one of the small bottles of mouthwash provided by the hotel to try to get the fur off her teeth. Borrowing Jake's comb, she determinedly attacked her hair and tried to tame it into some semblance of order. Finished she was glad to see that while she might not be at her most glamourous, she no longer looked like something the cat dragged in. Her dress was a lost cause, covered with dirt and sweat. She slipped it off and shrugged into a robe hanging on the back of the door. For a moment she closed her eyes and inhaled the scent of Jake that was clinging to the robe. Somehow, she found that the most comforting thing.

"I'm starving," she announced as she came back. She flinched her way to the chair beside his and helped herself to fruit and a croissant. Jake poured her some coffee. "Just black, please. Thanks for breakfast and the ibuprofen. And by the way, thanks for cleaning up my feet. Judging by what they look and feel like this morning, they must have been pretty bad last night." She took a grateful sip of coffee and snagged a pastry off the plate to nibble. "But now, I want to know what happened last night. I still can't quite believe that we were shot at."

Jake took a deep breath and told her about the man in the jacket and hat. How he had seen him at the military museum. How he thought he had been there when he picked up the pictures and again when they were at the restaurant last night.

"He's been following us? And you didn't tell me?"

"I wasn't sure that I wasn't just being paranoid. If I was overreacting, there wasn't any point in worrying you about something that wasn't real. The first shot last night made it pretty real. You went to sleep after we got back before I could tell you anything."

She looked at her bandaged feet. She had a vague memory of breaking down into a fit of the giggles after they got back last night. She shook her head to dispel the embarrassing thought. "So any idea why this man has been following us?"

"Not a clue. The only thing I can think of is that he somehow knows that we are looking for the hidden treasures. The only person that I know of who would be interested would be your professor. As far as we know, he is the only other person who knows about the treasure in enough detail to believe that it exists. It is too much of a coincidence that there would be a third person or group which would suddenly be searching for the treasure at this time."

"First of all, he isn't MY professor. And secondly, why would he care? Any glory that comes from us finding the treasure will reflect on him. Professors always get the credit for things their graduate students do."

Jake smiled grimly. "Sometimes, people are motivated by things other than recognition and prestige."

"But what else is there?"

Jake stood up and looked at her. "Rachel. Are you really this naïve? What motives ninety nine percent of people most of the time?" Rachel looked at him blankly. "Greed, Rachel. Greed."

"But these are historical artifacts; they are priceless and have no value on the open market. As soon as they are found, they will be claimed by the Maltese government, and they won't be able to be sold."

Jake shook his head and started to pace around the room. "He wouldn't sell them on the open market. There are plenty of collectors who are willing to pay lots of money for artifacts while overlooking that they have a dubious past."

The truth and reality of what Jake was saying hit Rachel heavily. She carefully placed her coffee mug on the table afraid that she might drop it.

"Let me be clear. You are saying that Dr. Bothell wants to find the artifacts and sell them." She didn't say it as a question. Her mind worked overtime as she thought through the situation. Dr. Bothell was always dressed in expensive, tailor-made suits, drove fancy expensive cars and she knew that he lived in a trendy, expensive part of the city. He had suddenly taken a holiday to Malta within days of her telling him of the treasure. She felt sick. "Dr. Bothell has been supplementing his university salary with black market trading."

"It is the only thing that makes sense."

Jake knelt in front of her chair and grasped her hands. "So we have a choice. We can take what we know to the authorities and let them take over the search or we keep looking. I'm not sure if the authorities will actually believe us but we can try."

Rachel shook her head.

Jake let out the breath he hadn't realized that he had been holding. He badly wanted to continue the search but at the same time, he didn't want for force her to do something she wasn't comfortable doing. "Okay then, let's say we find them first so that they don't get to the black market and everyone can enjoy them. We didn't look at the photos we took yesterday at the co-cathedral. Our after-dinner plans changed radically, although not by choice!"

Rachel managed a weak smile. "You're right. Let's beat him at his own game. We have the journal, and that is one thing that he doesn't have. That will make his job harder."

Jake retrieved his phone from the charger.

Opening up the photo roll, Jack enlarged and cropped the photos they had taken of the base of Zondardi's tomb. The panel they had identified was a rose marble background with a white inlay. The original inlay was the classic silhouette of a castle tower; a rectangle on end topped with three evenly spaced small squares. What had interested them was that over top of the inlay there were a series of deep scratches. They were difficult to see, and Rachel thought that someone in the past might have tried to polish them out.

"What does this look like to you?"

Rachel looked at the picture. "What if he was trying to keep the same theme as the original panel. Maybe this is meant to represent the outline of a building. There aren't really any castles per se on Malta so it would likely be one of the forts or another building important to the Knights." She picked up the local tourism magazine which seemed to be standard fare in every hotel room. She started to leaf through it. "There, that could be it." She squinted at it a bit and rotated the magazine. "Well, it's okay but not a great match." She continued flipping. "There," she said with satisfaction. "That's it." She laid the magazine down open to a picture of Fort St Angelo. Taking a pen, she drew around the silhouette of the Fort.

Jake picked it up and compared it with the photo. They matched almost perfectly. "You're good! I was worried that it would have been something that was destroyed during the war. But, you're right. This is almost a perfect match."

"What's the clue that goes with this?"

Jake picked up the journal and carefully found the spot. The journal was starting to show signs of wear. After being wrapped and stored for hundreds of years, the handling now was starting the cause the leather to crack. The pages continued to crumble around the edges, and they had been very careful about handling them.

" 'Originally of Mary, proven to withstand great strife, seek direction from the highest, let it point toward the stepping stone of color you seek.' Clears that right up, doesn't it?" Jake smiled at

Rachel. He was glad that they were able to focus on something productive at this point. Their earlier discussion about the professor had clearly distressed her. That in turn, on top of the dark shadows under her eyes put there from the events of last night, upset Jake. He realized that he had a need to take care of her. At this point, the only thing he could do was give her some distraction.

Rachel sat and thought for a while. "Well, nothing comes to mind immediately. I think I am going to have to do some research about Fort St Angelo. I don't know much about the structure itself. Its significance has always been in the role it played in the Great Siege."

"Okay, and where do we do that?"

Rachel smiled with pleasure. "Where else but the archives?"

12

Both Rachel and Jake were feeling tired and out of sorts. Rachel's feet felt as if the bottoms had been attacked by an angry cat and despite the fact she had loosened the straps on her sandals, the shoes now felt like they were two sizes too small. Earlier that day, they had discovered that while the archives of Malta had been kept in the Grand Masters' Palace but has since been moved to a site a short distance away. They had taken a cab as it was just too far to walk even if Rachel had felt up to it. It had taken some work to convince the clerk to let them take a look at the archives. Apparently they had a system in place which required preauthorization and after filling out the five page application form, it would take about a week for them to be granted that authorization. It had taken a mix of Rachel flirting with the clerk, overwhelming him with her knowledge of Malta and her beautiful smile to persuade him that he could bend the rules for her. They had then spent several hours pouring over dusty books to try to find some mention of Mary and Fort St Angelo. Jake had tired of it much sooner than Rachel but had stuck it out. He had great admiration for Rachel's ability to sit, read and take notes. And apparently, then remember everything she had read. Unfortunately, she just hadn't read anything helpful for their current situation. They had taken a break for lunch and then had returned to the hunt. Finally, Jake had had enough. Unable to find a cab, they had taken the bus back. Rachel usually didn't mind taking public transit, but the air conditioning was broken, and it seemed like every other resident of Valletta had opted to travel by bus, so she was now hot, distinctly sweaty and grumpy. Jake was not much better.

They had come back to the hotel to cool off and take a break. Jake opened the door to his room and fumbled for the light switch. He suddenly stopped walking and Rachel, who had been following him closely, slammed into his back.

"What…" Rachel bit down on her irritation, knowing that it stemmed from being hot and tired and their unsuccessful day.

Jake slowly stepped into the room. It was in complete disarray. His clothes had been pulled from the closet and strewn on the floor. They hadn't simply been thrown down but had been walked on as well. His suitcase had been torn open and left on the floor. The sheets from his bed were in a pile in the corner where they had been thrown, and the mattresses of both beds were now hanging precariously over the edges of the box springs.

"Oh my goodness, what happened Jake? Does your room attendant not like you?"

Jake stared in disbelief at the destruction of his property.

"I can't believe it. Who would do this? Why would they do this?"

Suddenly, Jake went to the closet. The safe was intact although it looked like someone had tried to open it with brute force. Jake punched in his code. As the door swung open, he sighed with relief. The journal was still there. "Trying to get the journal is why they would do this. We know that we are being followed. I think this counts as confirmation that they know about the journal and the treasure. And, that they are after it as well. They made this mess trying to find and steal the journal. Either that or they just assumed anything of value would be in the safe. Maybe they were simply trying to make it look like a robbery." He looked around again. "Not that anyone could believe that a simple robbery would involve this much destruction.

Rachel didn't want to believe that someone would go to the extreme of searching and destroying personal property just for the journal.

Jake checked the front pocket of his suitcase. The photos of the lipstick writing on the wall were gone. He tried to close his suitcase to see if it was still usable. It wasn't. He tossed it into the vicinity of the garbage can. "Well, that confirms it. The photos are gone. The only reason to take those is if you are looking for the treasure. Damn it."

Jake could feel himself getting angrier and angrier. The wanton destruction of his things was so unnecessary. As things, he didn't care about them. He was more worried that the level of violence had been designed to send a message. A message that he had no intention of heeding but he thought that Rachel should give up the search and go home. It was the only way he knew she would be safe.

"Look, Rachel. Maybe this is getting too intense. Maybe it isn't a good idea for us to be doing this. I think we should consider backing off and staying away from anything Order related. Maybe it is time to simply be tourists for the next few days until we have to head home."

Rachel looked at him. She walked over and stood directly in front of him. Taking his hands in hers, she looked into his face. "Jake, if I agree to stop looking, are you going to stop? Or are you simply going to continue without me?"

She had her answer when he looked away. She wrapped her arms around him as much to get comfort as to give it. "Jake, we are in this together. We are safer if we are together. From now on we simply carry the journal with us. We are careful not to get caught somewhere where there are only a few people especially if it is dark. Agreed?"

Jake held her. He laid his cheek on the top of her head. He allowed himself to relax and accept the comfort she offered. Then, he stepped back and took her by her shoulders. "Rachel, this is getting dangerous. You are important to me, and I don't want you to get hurt. Are you sure this is something that you want to do?"

Rachel smiled at him. "No Jake, I don't want to do it. I need to do it."

Jake sighed and pulled her back into an embrace. Some how he had known that she wouldn't give up the search. "Agreed."

13

The next day, Jake and Rachel sat at a small café overlooking the harbour. After the stress of the past two days, they had decided that they needed a bit of downtime to relax. As Rachel had said that morning, time to be normal. Being chased and shot at was definitely not normal. Having your hotel room ransacked and your belongings destroyed was definitely not normal. So after reporting the incident to the front desk and accepting many rounds of apologies from the front office staff, housekeeping and finally the general manager, they had escaped to do some shopping. The general manager assured them that housekeeping would do what they could to put the room to rights and repair any clothing they were able to. Having taken a few hours to replace some of Jake's wardrobe and toiletries, they were now taking a break.

Jake was pretty sure that left to his own devices, he could have replaced his clothes in about 20 minutes. Rachel, however, had insisted on visiting several different shops and at each one having him modeling things for her. Between her say so and input from the salespeople, Jake felt like he was being outfitted for a visit with royalty. He had tried to protest, but his efforts had been flicked aside by Rachel with a wave of her hand. After that, he had found it easier to be quiet and do as he was told. He looked down at the loose fitting pale blue linen shirt he was wearing and had to admit that she had much better taste than him. He probably would have hit the closest tourist shop and stocked up on Malta t-shirts.

Jake stretched his legs out in front of him and crossed his ankles. He sighed in satisfaction.
Rachel smiled at him. "You look like a cat who has just swallowed the canary."

"Well, if I were a cat, I would be purring like a V8 engine."

Rachel laughed, "Because you are sitting in the sunshine with a pint of beer about to appear or because we are finished your shopping?"

He surveyed the shopping bags scattered around him. "Both." He picked up the beer that the waitress had just placed before him.

Rachel smiled at the waitress as she put Rachel's wine on the coaster. "Men," she said. "They never appreciate the therapeutic effects of a good shopping spree."

The waitress eyed Jake with obvious approval. "Well, you are lucky your boyfriend would even go. Mine would have flat out refused, planted himself on the sofa in front of a game on TV and refused to move. Besides," she smiled coyly at Jake, "you look fantastic."

Rachel thought about correcting her assumption that Jake was her boyfriend, but given the way she was looking Jake up and down, she changed her mind. She reached across the table and interlaced her fingers with his.

Flashing a look at the waitress, she said, "Yes, I am lucky and don't I know it."

The server beat a hasty retreat at that point. Jake sat there a bit bemused by the exchange. Rachel's fingers were warm between his and the palm of her hand was soft as it pressed up against his. He couldn't say that he minded it there. He stroked his thumb over hers.

"What was that about?"

Rachel blushed and pulled her hand back, almost knocking over her wine in her haste.

"Sorry, I just didn't like how she was sizing you up like a hunk of meat. It just seemed...." she searched for the right word. "Offensive."

Jake smiled. "I can't say I minded."

Rachel turned away, embarrassed at her behavior. She wasn't sure why she had reacted like she had. It had just happened. Before she could analyze herself, she noticed a well-known figure walking toward them.

"Damn it." Rachel immediately felt the muscles in her shoulders tighten and a knot formed in her stomach. Now that they were sure someone was after them and that the professor was involved, it made her reaction stronger than ever.

Jake turned to look in the same direction. "Oh, here comes our favorite person." This time it was his turn to reach out and cover her hand. He gave it a reassuring squeeze. "Relax, it's okay. Don't let him have that power over you. He can't do anything to you. Look at me."

Rachel tore her eyes off the advancing figure and looked at Jake. He looked intently into her eyes. "Take a deep breath, that's it, one, then another one, good, now let your shoulders drop. You look like you are trying to cover your ears with your shoulders." He gave her hand one more squeeze and then leaned back into his chair.

Rachel concentrated on relaxing her muscles and slowing her breathing down. She knew from experience that she dealt with the professor better when she wasn't upset. She could hear his footsteps as he approached. She plastered a smile on her face.

"Good girl," Jake murmured.

"Rachel, my dear girl. Fancy running into you. I hope you are well."

Rachel turned toward her thesis supervisor. "Professor. How are you?"

To her dismay, he pulled over a spare chair from the table next to them and settled himself down at their table. Signaling the waitress, he ordered himself a glass of wine.

"My dear, I am just fine. But who is this young man? I don't believe we have met."

Rachel grudgingly introduced them.

"How lovely that you have found each other here on holidays. It is always more fun to travel with someone. I hope that Malta has been treating you well.   Have you been enjoying your days and evenings? I would think that the evenings are just about perfect for a romantic stroll through the streets of Malta. I trust you that you have been keeping to the safer areas."

Jake sharpened his look at him. He couldn't tell if the professor was asking this innocently out of genuine interest or if he was probing for information. Either way, Jake wasn't about to give him anything.

"We have been having a lovely time thank you. We have been trying new restaurants most nights, and you are quite correct. The evenings have been wonderful for walking."

Dr. Bothell continued on as if Jake had never spoken. "And how is your hotel? If I recall correctly, you said you were staying at the Hotel Grand Excelsior. I would expect that they would provide top notch service given they are a 5-star hotel. "

Rachel didn't think that she had told him where she was staying but at the same time, she couldn't be sure. So much had happened since their last encounter, the details of that conversation had faded.

Rachel opened her mouth to speak. Jake gripped her knee under the table. She was looking shocked and appalled, so Jake knew she was going to challenge him.

"It is a lovely hotel. The service is fantastic. I have never had such a clean and tidy room. The staff is very friendly, and the pool area is very relaxing." Jake waved a hand expansively. "And given the lower cost compared to staying in the city, it is well worth the short walk into town. And you, you are finding things with which to amuse yourself? Have you been to the War Museum yet? Visited the tunnels under the city? It is quite educational." Jake could give as good as he got.

"Yes, yes." The professor leaned back in his chair. Taking a sip of wine, he closed his eyes and took his time savoring the flavor. Rachel looked at Jake and rolled her eyes. "Ah, there is nothing like a cold glass of white wine on a hot sunny afternoon. What were you saying? Oh, yes, the tunnels and museum have much to teach us. In fact, this island has much to teach us." He took another sip and continued to pontificate. "The Knights of St John, such an impressive group. Dedicated on the one hand to helping the sick and poor and yet, on the other, developing a well run military machine. So interesting that they were able to do both despite the inherent contradictions in the positions."

"But," Rachel couldn't let that pass. "They were forced into developing the military branch during the Crusades to protect their hospitals and their good works. They didn't originally set out that way. The Knights Templar were more military initially, but they were unable to keep up the level of protection needed." Warming to the topic, Rachel leaned forward in her chair. "The Knights of St John were initially all about helping the sick and poor. They didn't want to have a military role."

"Rachel," She ground her teeth at the patronizing tone. "You should know by this time in your studies that the service alone didn't last very long before they developed a military arm. You should also recognize that over the years after they left Acre, they were pirates, ravaging ships and collecting prisoners and fortunes along their way. The altruistic order had a very definitely defined branch that thrived on violence." He finished off his glass of wine. "Ta ta for now. Enjoy your day and do keep out of the dangerous areas of the city. I wouldn't want anything to happen to you."

"Thank you Mr. Bottle, that is very kind of you."

Rachel saw the tightening of the muscles around the professor's eyes and the slight clench of his jaw. She knew how much it irritated him to not be addressed by his title. As he was constantly reminding his students, he had earned that title through hard work, and so he deserved to be recognized. Jake winked at her, and she knew that he had not called him doctor and gotten his name wrong on purpose. This thought gave a bounce to her spirit, and she was able to make her smile a bit more genuine.

"It's Doctor Bothell," the professor snapped back.

"Right, right, I am sorry. Names are not my strong suit. Well, have a good day." Jake turned back to Rachel effectively dismissing the professor.

Rachel saw him hesitate, not used to such unmannerly treatment, but he said nothing and turned on his heel to stroll away.

Rachel slumped back in her chair. "Unfortunately, what he is saying is, to a certain extent, true. The Knights developed two different groups. Some more focused on the service to the sick and poor and the others became pirates of the sea when they were in Rhodes and then again after moving to Malta. They would take on any Muslim ship, plundering and taking slaves and valuables. They used the excuse that the Muslims were taking Christian slaves and they were releasing them from slavery as a justification for their actions. But really they were just pirates. Given the slaves were chained in the bottom of the ship, they probably killed as many as they saved when ships sank before they could be boarded. And of course, all they did when they did capture a ship was to chain any non-Christian person to their oars. Not a stellar example of service to humanity."

Jake signaled for their bill. "Well, man's inhumanity to man based on color, religion, and pretty much any other definable difference is well documented through history. Regardless of religion, they were all just men and men will do terrible things in the name of God. Things that God would never sanction." He looked at the bill. "Do you realize that he stiffed us with the bill for his wine?"

Rachel snorted. "That sounds just like him. Do you think that he was hoping that we would tell him about the shooter and your room? Do you think that those questions confirms that he is involved?"

Jake slowly shook his head his gaze following the barely discernable figure of the professor in the distance. "I don't know. I really don't know. But it is really the only thing that makes sense."

14

After returning to the hotel to drop off Jake's bounty, they decided to take the ferry over to Fort St Angelo. They still didn't understand the clue, but as Jake pointed out, they couldn't go wrong by looking around the place where they were pretty sure they were supposed to find the next clue.

Both of them kept a sharp eye out for anyone who might be tailing them. Several people seemed to follow them off the ferry. They slowed down and hung back a bit, but everyone appeared to go on their way quickly and without caring about what the pair of them were doing.

They made their way down along the waterfront towards the Fort at the tip of the peninsula. Jake held Rachel back as she started to quicken her pace.

"Relax, let's just take things easy and take our time. We can keep an eye out for anything suspicious more easily that way." He took her hand in his. "Let's just look like any other couple out sightseeing while on holiday."

Rachel slowed and smiled at him. "You're right. I'm just anxious to see what is at the Fort."

By the time they had walked to the Fort, they both agreed that they hadn't seen anything or anyone that seemed out of place.

They walked up the long ramp to the front door. They paid the entrance fee and started to wander. The Fort was designed to have four batteries. The batteries would have housed the cannons and allowed for different stages of defense. The first battery was at sea level and was obviously the first line of defense. Each battery was a little higher up the hill and protected less territory. Each one would have allowed the Knights to retreat if necessary. However, they would have been able to re-establish a perimeter at the next battery level and resume a defense. Given that they weren't sure what they were looking for, Jake and Rachel followed the road which wound its way around the outside of the fort up towards the top. They passed the small building previously used as the magazine. As they reached the summit of the peninsula, they found themselves amongst some of the outbuildings. As they walked, they stopped to read the information placards explaining the role of each building. In the very center of the top plateau sat a chapel. In keeping with other buildings, it was built from sandstone and was relatively plain. Its function was advertised by the cross elevated above the front door.

Rachel tugged on Jake's sleeve. "Look, a chapel. Maybe it is named after Mary. Maybe that is where we are supposed to look." She let go of his hand and ran to the chapel. Jake saw her shoulder's droop as she read the information placard. "This isn't it. This is the Chapel of St Anne."

They both stood back and looked at the building. Scaffolding surrounded the door and the front wall. Workers were moving in and out of the building carrying trowels and other equipment. Some sort of renovation was taking place.

Jake fished the journal out of his backpack. He turned to the clue. "Rachel, the clue says formerly of Mary. Not of Mary. Maybe this is the 'in the ground, on the ground' type of clue. We aren't supposed to take it at face value." He gestured towards the chapel. "Don't they change the names of churches and chapels over time depending on who is in control of the land? Is it possible that this used to be a chapel of Mary, not Anne?"

Rachel's eyes started to brighten. "Let's find out. Excuse me," she made her way over to one of the workers. "Can you tell me if this chapel was ever dedicated to Mary instead of Anne?"

Jake could see that the worker was admiring the view as he looked at Rachel. His gaze still hadn't reached her face when he shook his head. "Ma nifhimx." He gestured towards the entrance. "Tiegħu magħluqa. Inti ma tistax tmur fil."

Jake walked over. "I don't think he speaks English. And if my interpretation is correct, I think he is saying the chapel is closed. Come on, let's find someone we can ask. Maybe they will let us in anyway. Maybe those credentials of yours as a researcher will come in handy!"

"Bye tajba mara pretty." The worker accompanied his final comment with a wolf whistle.

"What is it with you men? You just can't stop yourselves from commenting on a woman. And when I say commenting, I mean reducing her to a sex object."

Jake held his hands up in mock surrender. "It wasn't me. Me, I haven't noticed how beautiful you are and how your smile is so attractive. Me, all I know is that you are clearly the smartest person here. For all I've noticed, you could be terribly homely. I cannot be held responsible for the rest of my gender, philistines that they all are."

Rachel laughed. "Okay. I won't hold it against you. Excuse me." Rachel called to a guide who was saying goodbye to her group.

"Can I help you?" The guide acknowledged Rachel's call but quickly turned her eyes on Jake. She smiled coyly at him.

"Yes, please. Can you tell me if the Chapel of St Anne was ever named after Mary?" Rachel asked.

"Yes, yes it was. Before the Knights arriving, it was dedicated to

Mary. After they had arrived, they rededicated it to St Anne." She moved a bit closer to Jake, failing to even look at Rachel as she answered her question. "I'm afraid it is closed right now for repairs. If you can come back again next month, it will have reopened. I would be more than happy to arrange a private tour for you." She slid a hand down Jake's arm. Clearly, her invitation for a private tour did not include Rachel.

Rachel wedged herself between Jake and the guide. "That is very kind of you but unfortunately, we won't be here then. I am a researcher doing my Ph.D. in History. Would it be at all possible for us to have a peek inside now? I promise we won't disturb the work at all."

The guide, having decided that Jake was not responding as she had hoped, drew herself up and turned to Rachel. She was significantly less friendly as she replied to her. "Absolutely not. It is closed and not open to the public. You will simply have to return another time. Now, if you will excuse me. It is time for my lunch."

Jake could barely contain himself until the guide was out of earshot. He was laughing. "Men! You have a complaint about men! That woman was far worse and more obvious than that worker. Men. What is it with you women that you think men are the only ones who turn people into sex objects?" He continued to laugh.

Rachel started to respond hotly but then realized how futile her argument would be. Ruefully she chuckled herself. "Okay, so the timing on that wasn't the best." She sobered. "But, what are we going to do? How are we going to get inside?"

Jake moved into the shade under a small tree and sat on a rock. "Didn't she say something about lunch time?" He checked his watch. "It is currently about ten to one. By my estimation, that means in about ten minutes, the crew is going to break for lunch as well." He patted the rock beside him. "Why don't you take a load off until then?"

Rachel sat. "You are so smart."

"See, even you have to admit that I am more than a handsome face!"

Sure enough, in a few minutes, they could see that the workers were slowing down. Rachel could only hope that they would go elsewhere for their lunch. They emerged from the chapel in twos and threes. Some of them starting walking down the road and were obviously headed out for lunch. Others had lunch boxes and bottles of water. Rachel held her breath as they paused outside the chapel. Fortunately, the angle of the sun was such that the only other shade on the plateau was at the back of the chapel. The men made their way to the spot and settled in to eat. Rachel was ready to hop up and get going, but Jake held her back.

"Wait. Let them get comfortable. Once they have settled in, they will be less likely to notice us."

After what seemed like forever for Rachel, Jake quietly stood up. Together they picked their way towards the chapel trying to avoid making noise but at the same time trying to avoid looking suspicious. The workers were deep into conversation and were apparently debating the pros and cons of some sports player. Jake and Rachel slipped into the chapel. They stood just inside and allowed their eyes to adjust to the dimness. As they adjusted, it became evident that the roof of the chapel was being worked on. Despite the scaffolding that filled the sanctuary, the beauty of the chapel was still obvious. Empty except for the construction debris, the chapel's ceiling rose in multiple vaults. The vaults along the side of the chapel tended to be barrel vaults. Others were the more complicated groin vaults. The groin vaults appeared as if they were beautiful folds of stone coming together to support the roof. The archways of each vault appeared to be edged by lighter sandstone. Rachel wasn't sure if this was the case or if those areas had simply been cleaned. The arches and ribs of each vault continued down into either the walls or square pillars which formed the corners and supports of the room. A single round support stood in the middle of the chapel holding everything together. For several minutes they simply admired the incredible feat of construction the chapel roof represented. Then, Rachel and Jake began to move around the room trying to make sense of the clue.

"It says highest; do you think that means it is on the ceiling?" Rachel started to climb one of the scaffolding units. Jake grabbed her.
"What do you think you are doing?"
"Climbing, what does it look like?"

"Let me do that." He tried to tug her down.

"What, I can't climb scaffolding? You climb that one over there. Maybe the clue is in the top of that vault."

What she said made sense. If the clue was on the ceiling, then there were several vaults to inspect, and it made more sense for them to split up. Both of them climbed to the top and started looking at each piece of stone. Suddenly one of the workers entered the chapel. Rachel and Jake froze. They each tracked the progress of the worker not sure if this meant that lunch break was over or what. He looked around and then wandered over to a bag in the corner to retrieve his thermos. Jake and Rachel looked at each other with relief as he left. They resumed their search. Rachel marveled over how each stone fit exactly with the surrounding stones. The craftsmanship and skill was astounding especially when everything would have been done by hand.

Half an hour later, after climbing up and down scaffolding through out the chapel, they met down on the floor in the middle. "Anything?" Jake shook his head. "Me too. Absolutely nothing. Each stone looked exactly the same. Which, when you think about it, is pretty remarkable, but doesn't help our search."

Rachel leaned again the middle support and looked up at the ceiling. Suddenly, both of them looked at each other. They spoke at the same time.

"Do you think it could be?"

"That's it!"
They turned and looked at the support Rachel was leaning on. It was the only circular post in the building and was supporting the

highest point of the roof. The post was the only support which was not square and not made of yellow sandstone. It was red. Rachel circled it running her hand over the smooth surface. She continued to circle looking lower and lower on the pillar to double check for anything that might give them more information. Jake climbed the adjacent scaffolding to do the same on the upper half.

Rachel reached the bottom. "There is nothing down here. It is completely smooth. Anything up there?"

Jake clambered down. "Nothing other than smooth polished stone. It is beautiful."

"X'qed tagħmel hawn? You no allowed. Closed."

In their delight at the find and their concentration, they had forgotten to listen for the workers. Lunch time was now over and the men stood arrayed around the entrance of the chapel. One of the men, obviously the foreman, stood out in front. He was clearly not pleased with their presence in the chapel. Rachel stepped forward with her most beguiling smile.

"We are so sorry; it is just so beautiful we couldn't resist taking a look." Moving steadily towards the exit, she motioned Jake to follow. "You are doing such a great job of restoring or renovating or what ever you are doing. Please keep up the great work and thank you, all you, for doing it. It is just beautiful. You should be very very proud of the work you do and of the country. We love Malta, it is just the most wonderful country and you are all so friendly and accommodating."

The workers parted around them as they moved through to the exit. Rachel was a bit worried when she saw that the foreman was on a radio, but she continued. As her long speech in English fell over the workers, she and Jake worked their way quickly out and into the courtyard. She continued to talk until they were well away from the chapel.

"Thank you." With one final wave, the two of them continued to walk as quickly as they could away from the chapel.

Jake looked at her. "That was impressive."

"Sometimes you just have to use what you have." Rachel said with her bright beautiful smile. "Now, let's get out of here before whoever the foreman alerted shows up to escort us off the premises!"

15

"The Tower rises and points the way to where the bees dance and time blows freely."

Jake and Rachel were once again sitting down by the water at the hotel. The journal and all of their paper notes were spread around on the table. Their morning coffee cups were carefully anchoring the sheets in the light breeze. Rachel leaned back in her chair and closed her eyes. She enjoyed the heat of the sun on her face, and she turned her head towards the cool breeze providing a nice balance to the heat.

"Perfect," she said. "Just perfect. The temperature is perfect; the setting is so beautiful." She opened her eyes to take in the view of the three cities across the bay. "Just perfect. Except, of course, for having your room broken into, being chased around the city and being shot at." She shivered at the thought of what might have happened.

Jake still couldn't believe that it had escalated to a point where someone was willing to hurt or even kill them to stop their search. Over dinner last night Rachel had talked about the stories she had heard from colleagues about how competitive archeological digs and the search for artifacts could be. She had always taken their stories with a grain of salt, never truly believing that things could get violent.

Jake rested his hands on the table. "Well, it means that we have to be more careful. Clearly, your professor is willing to go to pretty great lengths to get to this treasure first. I will admit that when I first thought about this trip, I never in a million years would have thought anything like this would or could happen. I am sorry that I dragged you into this."

Jake looked at her. She had left her hair loose and the breeze was blowing it back from her face. Her profile was outlined against the bright blue sky. She had the cutest little up turned nose that gave her face a mischievous look even in repose. He was struck yet again by how beautiful she was. He knew that she was unaware of her beauty and he found that this simply made her more attractive. She turned to face him and laid her hand over his. He could feel the heat of her hand on his. He looked at her fingers, how they appeared to be so fragile but he knew that in that delicate hand, there was a lot of strength. He covered her fingertips with his thumb.

"And how exactly did you drag me into this?" Rachel felt the pressure of his thumb as a current that ran through her hand and up her arm. Her heart started to beat a bit faster, and she lost her train of thought. She could feel the roughness of his skin on hers and knew that it was roughness that came from hard work. She wondered at how quickly he had come to mean so much to her. It felt like she had known him for years rather than the better part of a week. Suddenly she realized that Jake was looking at her expectantly.

"Right, what was I saying?" She gave herself a mental shake. "Jake, you didn't drag me into this, I practically threw myself into it. I wouldn't have left you to do it alone. Assuming that he doesn't want to find the treasure for the treasures sake but for profit, it becomes even more important for us to find it first. Anything that is out there belongs to the country of Malta and its people. It is part of their history and their place in the world." She squeezed his hand gently and then before she made a fool of herself by clinging to his hand and begging him to hold her, she drew her hand back and picked up the journal. "This means that we have to figure out the next clue. So, do you think that the important aspect of the pillar in the chapel is that it was circular or that it was the only red stone in the building?"

They debated back and forth about which of the two would have been the clue referred to by Rafael. Either way, having only two unique features would likely make it easier to figure out which was important.

"The tower must be one of the watchtowers." Rachel mused. "Or, I suppose, it could be a tower on a building. I don't think they had anything that would be considered a tower actually on a building unless it was a turret. I don't consider turrets to be towers. If we assume that the important feature is that it is circular, then we would be looking for a circular tower. If we assume that the important feature of the pillar in the chapel being its colour, do you think that means the tower was painted red? Or that it is red inside, maybe one room is red and looking out the window points the way?" She sighed as Jake started to laugh. "I guess it would be too easy for one of them just to have a big bright red arrow pointing out the right direction wouldn't it?"

Jake was still chuckling. "Yes, yes, I think it would. Nothing seems to have been that simple. Come, on. Let's go." He stood up and started to gather all of the papers together.

"Go where?" Rachel asked, puzzled. "We don't know where to go."

Obediently, she stood and picked up her bag. Jake was already heading towards the hotel. She quickly followed him. By the time she caught up with him, he was already in negotiations for renting a car.

"Yes sir, you can pick it up from the upper parking lot. You can keep the keys for as long as you would like and we will add the charges to your bill. May I have your driver's license please?"

As the concierge continued to complete the paperwork, Jake turned to Rachel.

"We are going on a road trip."

"Okay," she said slowly. "Where exactly is this road trip going?"
Jake shrugged. "I don't know. We will figure that out later."

Rachel only shook her head. If he wanted to spend his money on renting a car, who was she to argue? To her, it seemed like a waste of time to be driving aimlessly around the island hoping that something would pop out and scream that it was the answer to the next clue. She stifled her reluctance and followed him to the car.

Jake got in on the driver's side and handed a map to her as she sat and buckled herself in.

He could tell she was thinking. She got the cutest little line between her eyebrows when she was upset or thinking hard. Right now, he wanted to assume it was because she was thinking but he was pretty sure it was because she was irritated.

"Look, Rachel, I couldn't exactly say to you in front of the concierge that we were going to go on a road trip to look at watch towers. That seemed a bit too much like advertising and asking for trouble." He carefully backed up. Looking over his shoulder he could see two large men getting into a small green car. "As it is, I think we have a tail." He shook his head. "I can't believe that I just said 'I think we have a tail.' Even more, I can't believe that it is true."

He headed up the driveway. Turning right, he reminded himself that he needed to drive on the opposite side of the road than he was used to. He checked his rear-view mirror. Sure enough, the little green car turned the same way. He drove casually along the road knowing that he was going to have to do something to lose the tail. If he didn't, he might as well have shouted out to the entire lobby where they were going.

Rachel was twisted around in her seat trying to look. Jake pushed her back around.

"Play cool. It will be easier to try to lose them if they think we don't know they are there. Here's the map, start looking at how best to see as many of the watch towers as possible. I will look after this."

He turned randomly left and right and circled a roundabout three times as if he didn't know which way he wanted to go. The green car fell back a few cars but stuck with them. He exited the roundabout when he could see that a horse and buggy was up ahead. The carriage had two tourists more interested in each other than the scenery. There was oncoming traffic but if he timed it right...

"Hold on."

He pushed the accelerator to the floor hoping the car had enough power to do what he needed. The car shot forward and he shifted up a gear.

"Jake...you won't get around in time. There is a car coming. Jake!"

"I see it."

Jake cut out around the horse and buggy and pulled back into his lane with inches between his right front fender and the bumper of the oncoming car. He was aware of the startled faces of the tourists as they whizzed by, the fist-shaking of the horse cabbie as well as the horns of the oncoming cars. He slowed only slightly, trying to put distance between them and the green car. Checking the rear-view mirror, Jake saw exactly what he had hoped to see. The green car was stuck behind the buggy as there was now a steady stream of oncoming traffic. He could see the passenger with his head and shoulders out of the window shouting at the cabbie. After rounding the next corner, he reduced his speed to the limit trying to blend back into the traffic. He took the next four turns at random but at the same time trying to head towards the coast. Finally, when he was sure he had lost them, he pulled off onto the side of the road.

Rachel was white faced and gripping the door handle as if the door was about to fall off the car. "D-o-n-'-t y-o-u e-v-e-r do that again! You could have killed us or the people in the buggy or in the oncoming car or all of us for that matter." Her voice increased in volume with every word.

Jake reached across and pulled her into his shoulder. "It's okay. We are safe, so is everyone else. I used to race cars when I was a teenager. I wouldn't have done it if I hadn't been sure that I could do it without hurting anyone." He failed to mention that if the car hadn't responded as he needed it to, things might have been different. "Honey, we had to get rid of our tail." Jake could feel her shaking against him. He drew her back from him. Her hair fell over her eye and he smoothed it behind her ear. "Look at me." She raised tear-filled blue eyes to his. "We are okay. We know that these guys play for keeps. We needed to get rid of them or who knows what they would have been willing to do. Okay?" She gave a shaky nod. He pulled her in for another hug.

"Look, I know this has been a lot. If you want to quit, tell me. We will walk away. If you have had enough, we will call it quits."

Rachel closed her eyes and tried to relax against him. She drew comfort from the solid, steady heartbeat under her ear and the strength of the arms around her. She sat up and wiped her eyes. "No, we need to continue. I'm okay, it was just unexpected. Let's go before they find us again."

"That's my girl. Now, as Chief Navigator, how to we get to the closest watchtower?"

She opened the map. It was shaking so hard he was surprised that she could read anything.

"Where are we now?" Rachel peered out the window to find the closest street signs. "Okay, so, we are here." She pointed to a spot on the map. "We need to get to here." She pointed at another place. Jake saw her start to settle as she planned their route.

Jake pulled back onto the road to follow her directions.

16

"All right, let's visit one more tower and then call it a day."

Wearily, Rachel got out the map yet again. After driving for what seemed like hours, negotiating the twisting streets which often seemed to have no room for one car to travel on it, let alone one in each direction, stopping to ask for directions after getting lost for the umpteenth time, and visiting 5 watchtowers, the two of them were starting to get discouraged and grumpy. The sum total of their efforts had been one watch tower that wasn't open to the public, one tower which had only one window which pointed out to sea and from which nothing else could be seen, (Rachel had pointed out that it made sense for that to be the case given that they were to watch for invading forces but by that time, Jake was tired of driving, hiking up hills, climbing stairs in the towers and didn't really care about logic.), two towers which had been restored and while they had multiple windows (which Jake pointed out was really a reasonable thing to do as it allowed for a cross breeze), there was nothing red, reddish, or any other colour other than the sporadic grey of granite or the constant yellow of sandstone, on, in or around the buildings. One other tower had been temporarily closed to the public due to its state of repair but Jake had, as he called it, maneuvered his way through the boarded up lower window to do recognizance. But there had been nothing other than a collapsed roof and deteriorating stairs. None of them had been circular. The only other thing they hadn't seen all day was the little green car and for this, they were grateful.

Now, they were headed for their last tower of the day.

They topped the hill that led down into the valley holding the village of Cirkewwa. They could see Gozo and Comino off in the distance.

"Oh, Jake, it's beautiful. Look at the light on the water. It's so pretty. You can see the ferry crossing over from Gozo. We really should do that when we get this all solved." She sighed and said wistfully, "It would be lovely to be able just to be tourists and do some of the touristy things. I hear that Gozo is known for its honey. Apparently, the island used to be covered with thyme, you know, the herb, and so the bees make honey from the nectar of their flowers. We really should…" She grabbed the dashboard as Jake hit the brakes.

He pulled the car off onto the edge of the road. They had just rounded a corner coming down the hill.

"You have got to be kidding me."

"What?" Rachel turned to look where Jake was pointing.

"Are you seeing what I am seeing?"

"I don't believe it."

The two of them spoke over top of each other. They turned at looked towards one another and started to laugh. Needing the comic relief, they found that each time they started to get it together again, they looked out the window and started to laugh again. Finally, Rachel pulled out a Kleenex to mop up the tears from her cheeks. She was holding her stomach. "I can't laugh anymore, my stomach hurts."

Jake smiled with pure joy. "Well, I take it back. I guess sometimes it can be easy."

Standing tall and proud a short distance down the hill and off to the side of the road stood their last watch tower of the day. A red watch tower.

They pulled into the parking lot just as the attendant for the tower was starting to lock the door. Rachel had flown out of the car before Jake had gotten it into park.

"Oh, please, please don't say we can't go in. Please don't say it's closed."

"Sorry, ma'am. We close at 5 o'clock. We are closed tomorrow, but we will be open again at 9 o'clock the morning after." The attendant turned back to check that the door was securely locked.

"No, no, no, no, please we have to get in," she was clinging to the attendant's arm. The contrast between the elation of finding the red tower and the thought that they were unable to go in dropped her mood like a stone. Despairing that they would ever solve the mystery and overwhelmed by the events of the last several days, this roadblock proved to be the last straw and she broke down into tears.

The attendant looked at her aghast.

"There, there, it's okay honey." Jake put his arm around her shoulders, drew her back from the attendant and gave her a squeeze. "Your grandfather would have understood. You tried." He pressed a kiss to her temple and then turned to the attendant. "Sorry about the wife. She is a bit overwrought. You know how a woman can get." He tried for his best southern drawl. "We came all the way from America to see this spot. I had to do business in London, you know, and being so close, well, we thought that we might as well squeeze in a day trip to Malta. You see, her grandfather lived in Malta. He used to come and climb the Red Tower and pretend to be a Knight when he was a little boy. He told all these stories to the little woman here and after he died last month, she suddenly had this obsession with seeing this spot." He shook his head. The attendant was looking at them in shock as Jake's words rolled over him. Rachel was continuing to cry in Jake's arms.

"There, there, baby, it's okay, you never wanted to see this before, so you'll get over it. I'm sure we can find some pictures somewhere to make up for it." He spoke over her head. "We have to leave first thing tomorrow morning; I have to get back to work and then there are the kids. We left them with her parents but no one wants to look after six kids for too long. You understand. John Junior, the oldest you know, is having his eighth birthday next week. We wanted to have some stories for the party but well, he'll just have to adjust."

The attendant's jaw had dropped at the revelation that there were six children under the age of eight waiting for them and he nodded slowly, either in shock or sympathy.

Rachel, finally realizing what Jake was up to, played her part. She lifted her head and wailed. "The children, I told them that I would see Grandpa's old playground. Susie and Jonny will be so disappointed." She started to sob even louder.

The attendant's expression turned to shock to horror to panic. Hastily he unlocked the door. "Okay, but only five minutes."

He made as if to follow them as they entered. Jake stopped and put his hand on his shoulder. "It might be better if we did this alone. All that grief you know."

The attendant nodded again wisely and with obvious relief, stepped back outside.

Rachel started up the steps and started to giggle. "Six children?"

"Here I thought you would take offense to the 'little woman' comment. Anyway, it worked didn't it? Now hurry we don't have a lot of time."

They climbed to the top and entered the room. This room also only had one opening but clearly visible through the arrow slit was the island of Gozo.

"Let me take a bearing."

Rachel fished through her purse and pulled out the compass she always carried. She stood in front of the window. She wasn't sure which direction she was supposed to be looking, so she placed the compass in the center of the window and took a reading out to the left which crossed the sill at the corner of the slit. She repeated it on the right side. Somewhere in that range would be the place that they would want. Luckily the window was just a slit for firing arrows, so the angle between the two measurements was small. She knew that the farther away from the tower they got, however, even with the narrow angle, the greater the area that could be involved. She was a bit worried that the spot was going to be underwater. If it was, it would likely be impossible to find. In the centuries since the treasure had been hidden, the tides would have transformed the floor of the ocean. The artifacts themselves, would have become covered in coral and crustaceans. She shook off the thought. There wasn't anything she could do about it if it was submerged.

"There isn't anything else here that I can see." Jake was scouring the stone walls trying to find any other clue that might be there to help them narrow down the line of sight they were supposed to be using. Rachel began to scan the walls herself. For the most part, they were smooth and appeared to have weathered the years extraordinarily well. Here and there, some love-struck person had felt that they had the right to carve their and their beloved's initials in the walls. "Idiot," thought Rachel as she saw these. She knew that many people didn't know or care about the significance of historical monuments and would see this only as pile of stones on which they felt they had to leave their mark.

"Hello, are you done? I don't mean to rush you at all, but well, it is after five. I really have to lock up and go."

The attendant was making his way up the stairs. Rachel quickly pocketed the compass and the notes she had made.

"Ready sweetheart?" He remembered at the last minute to drawl the words.

"Yes, darling. Oh, I am so happy. Thank you so much, I so appreciate this. I will be sure to tell little Jonny and Susie about the kind man who let us in to see the spot their beloved grandpa used to play."

She burbled her way down the stairs to the ground floor. "I can't thank you enough," she flung her arms around the bewildered attendant and rolled her eyes at Jake who was standing behind them laughing silently. She continued to spout nonsense until she and Jake were back in the car and pulling away from the tower.

"I never was one to make idle conversation," she said.

"But you are so good at it, I thought you had had lots of practice." joked Jake. Rachel swatted him on his arm.

"I certainly have since arriving on Malta, between construction workers and tower attendants I seem to have had lots of experience!"

As Jake drove back towards Valetta, they both fell silent as they sat and reflected. Jake was filled with excitement and awe in equal amounts. Excitement that they were on the brink of solving another clue and at the same time a bit shocked and amazed that they had been able to get as far as they had. He worried a bit about what might be next. He wondered how they would deal with the professor. He was sure that the professor wasn't going to give up easily. The fact that they had lost his men today didn't mean much. It meant even less when Jake realized that while he and Rachel hadn't known about the Red Tower, it was clearly a well-established monument on the island. One that the professor likely knew about or would have no trouble finding out about. He sighed and turned his attention back to the road. They would deal with what came next tomorrow. Tonight they would celebrate their success.

17

Jack checked his backpack and added in his flashlight. Packed already were a long sleeve black shirt and his new black jeans. He had also packed a Swiss army knife he had purchased earlier. It wasn't much in terms of protection, and certainly was nothing against a bullet, but he felt better knowing he had it. He had packed a couple of protein bars and some water. He wasn't sure what the day would bring, but they had decided that they had best be prepared for a long day and the possibility of some nighttime adventuring.

Yesterday, after a celebratory dinner and an uneventful stroll along the waterfront, they had called it an early night and agreed to meet for breakfast to discuss the next steps.

Rachel had been able to cajole a detailed map of Malta which included all three islands from the concierge. Over breakfast, Rachel had drawn on the map the area encompassed by the coordinates she had taken at the tower. Fortunately, vast majority of the area was ocean. Because the clue commented on the bees and the wind, they made the assumption that the next clue would be actually on the island of Gozo. While both of them agreed that it was unlikely that the treasure had been buried at sea, they still had concerns that it may have been. However, at this point, neither of them were licensed or equipped to scuba dive so there was nothing they would be able to do about it if it turned out that it was. They were both relieved when it became evident that the outermost portion of the reading on one side, just reached the edge of Gozo. Specifically, it had just reached the Azure Window, a famous tourist site. They were planning on heading out there today to see what they could find. Jake was prepared for a long day and had tried to cover all his bases.

A knock on his door brought him back to the present. He grabbed his jacket and opened the door.

"Ready?" Rachel also had her backpack filled with dark clothes. She was wearing a pretty outfit designed to look like they were simply going off for a day of touring.

"I sure am." Jake started to let the door swing closed. "Shoot, the car key."

He caught the door.

"Can you hold this?"

Rachel held the door while he went back to grab the key from the dresser.

"Okay, now I am ready."

The sun was high in the sky. No clouds were visible. As they drove they could see the glint of sun on the tops of the waves creating a look of multiple winking diamonds on dark blue velvet. The breeze provided respite from the intense heat of the sun and they drove with the windows down. They retraced their steps from the day before and headed back towards the red tower. It was a short distance from there where they would pick up the ferry to Gozo. They had decided to take the car rather than taxis or buses as it would give them more freedom and flexibility. Jake kept an eye out for a tail but was unable to identify anyone who might be following. Certainly, he didn't see either of the two men or the green car from yesterday. Either he wasn't skilled enough at catching out tails, today's tail was better than yesterday's, or they were in the free and clear. Jake choose to believe that they were clear.

The trip to the island was uneventful. They had spent the ferry ride on the deck pointing out different points of interest to each other and enjoying the day. Once off the ferry and back in the car, Rachel again assumed the role of navigator to get them to the Azure Window. They wound their way around the small island. The landscape was quite different from the main island with fields of green and increased evidence of agriculture. The topography was rugged and had more hills. The streets were the same twisty, narrow lanes that made driving a challenge, although as Jake pointed out, it made driving on the opposite side of the road to what he was used to much easier. He felt like he was simply driving down the middle!

Rachel caught her breath as they crested the final hill. Spread below them were broad sandstone dunes, a beautiful aquamarine ocean, and the Azure Window. It was postcard perfect. The Azure Window was essentially a flat-topped arch of which one leg was set off in the ocean while the other was attached to the mainland. The Arch created a beautiful window through which the gorgeous water of the Mediterranean Sea could be seen. The arch had been formed through years of erosion by the waves. It was a beautiful sight.

They wound their way down the hillside and parked the car. There were a lot of tourists but most came by tour bus, so there were not a lot of cars. Jake and Rachel joined in the picture taking and exploring. They wandered over the sandstone bluffs and watched the waves crashing against the shoreline. They walked down towards the inland lake. In reality, it was a small inlet from the ocean which washed in and out under a low arch. The opening was underwater during high tide. The lake had small boats which the tourists could take out and float under the arch when it was low tide.

For a time, they forgot why they were there. They simply enjoyed each others company and watched the antics of the other tourists. They took their own share of selfies and took turns taking pictures of each other. Once, another tourist asked them if they would like a picture of themselves as a couple. After blushing, Rachel had enthusiastically agreed. Finally, they decided to have lunch at the small restaurant.

After enjoying a delicious goat cheese and honey salad and sharing some roasted rabbit, they began to think more about why they were there.

"If my measurements are correct," said Rachel, "the farthest point that would be included in the arch from the watch tower would be just on the other side of the crest of that hill." She gestured to the hill out behind the restaurant. "But I don't think I can narrow it down more than that."

Jake surveyed the territory that included. "Well, it isn't that much land. We walked over much of the flat top of the cliffs across from the Window. There didn't seem to be much there unless there are caves along the water's edge. If that's the case, then those aren't going to be easily reached. The Window's arch itself is out of bounds, although it wouldn't have been during the time of the Knights, obviously. And then there is only the area around the inland lake and then the hill behind the restaurant." He thought for a while. "I ready don't think that he would have hidden things in the cliff side below where we walked. That would seem a bit risky to me. Too much risk of erosion from the sea I would think." Rachel agreed.

"Let's take a walk."

Rachel complimented the amazing meal and wonderful local honey to their waitress. She added a jar to their bill.

Once outside, they treated themselves to an ice cream cone and sat on a rock facing the Window and the adjacent hill. They agreed that the only place that made sense was somewhere on the hillside. They both secretly hoped that all their assumptions were true. Coming this far and then not being able to complete the adventure, somehow seemed unfair. Having finished her cone, Rachel used her phone to take photos of the area. Given the beauty of the area, she didn't have to act like a tourist; she just was one.

When she was satisfied, she had captured all of the areas they were interested in. They sat together and went through them one by one. They enlarged each photo and systematically looked for changes in color, texture or other signs that there might be a hiding place. "There." Jake pointed to a dark shadow on one of the photos. "What does that look like to you?"

Rachel shoved her glasses further up her nose. "A shadow, no, it's not a shadow, it's the mouth of a cave."

"I agree." Jake slowly reduced the enlarged photo taking note of landmarks as they appeared. The cave seemed to be at the top of hill behind the restaurant and to their right. Both of them surveyed the hillside trying not to be obvious about it.

"There it is. Can you see it?" Jake didn't want to point. "There is a little scraggly bush just to the left of the opening. And below that, there is a large boulder."

"I see." replied Rachel. "Now what?"

"Now we wait until dark."

Not wanting to look like they were hanging around the Azure Window with nothing to do, they had spent the afternoon exploring other parts of Gozo. Between the two of them, they had felt like they were being followed but had been unable to agree on who or what was following. Jake wasn't sure if that meant that there were two people following them or if one or both of them were wrong.

As darkness fell, they made their way back towards the Window. Jake pulled the car into a parking lot for a nearby watchtower. It had the advantage of being partway up the hill they were going to climb but more importantly, it was isolated. If they were being followed, it would be easy to see them coming.

"We walk from here. Let's get changed."

Jake stepped out of the car and moved around to the back. He pulled his shirt and pants out of the backpack. Stripping down to his boxers, he quickly changed into the dark clothes. He resisted the urge to look and see what state of undress Rachel was in.

"Done," Rachel called out softly.

They made their way up the hillside to the mouth of the cave. It was a painstakingly slow process. The grade was relatively steep and the footing uncertain. It took them at least twice as long to make the trip than Jake had anticipated. He worried with every step that someone was tracking them. Even with their dark clothing, he was sure they stood out from the lighter ground like a beacon. Easy targets to follow and easy targets to shoot. He was only grateful that Rachel seemed unaware of the danger they could potentially be in.

Finally, they made it to the entrance of the cave. Jake was relieved that there actually was a cave. He had started to worry that they were wrong and that it had been just a shadow in the photo after all. Rachel was breathing heavily. She dusted the dirt from her hands and knees. Parts of the climb had been steep enough that she had done it on all fours.

"Well, I think that counts as my exercise for the day!"

Jake chuckled. "Just wait until we have to go down!"

Rachel looked back over her shoulder. She pulled a face. "Right, I forgot about that. We didn't bring a rope or anything like that did we?"

Jake shrugged off the backpack he had been carrying. "Nope sorry, but I did bring these." He fished out two small flashlights and handed one to her.

Jake played his flashlight over the surface of the cave. It was just big enough for him to stand up in the opening. The cave extended about ten feet back into the cliff with the roof getting lower and lower. Great, Jake thought. With my luck, the clue is going to be on the back wall and I am going to have to be lying down to see it.

The walls were surprisingly smooth. There were outcroppings and rough patches here and there but nothing like they had seen down in the tunnels under the museum.

"You start on that side by the front and I'll start on the other side. We can meet in the middle at the back. Let me know if you find something."

Rachel nodded her agreement and moved to her side. They carefully scanned the walls with their flashlights.

"What do you think we are looking for?" asked Rachel after a few minutes of searching. "A drawing, an arrow, a map, or is it even on the walls? Maybe there is something about how the stones are placed on the ground."

Jake continued his search. He shook his head.

"I don't think so. Raphael wouldn't have known how long it would be before someone came to look for the treasure. He would have left something that would be more permanent than a set of rocks on the ground. He wouldn't have risked an animal or time or even an earthquake being able to ruin the clue. He wanted these things to be found, just by the right people and not easily."

Rachel grudgingly agreed and turned back to her side of the cave.

She shone her light over the wall and caught the hint of something as she passed over an area. The rest of the walls were yellow with some gray tones and matte. There was nothing really shiny on them. She moved the beam over the area again. There it was. Just a hint of a glint, so slight that if she hadn't been searching for it, she would have missed it.

"Jake, I think I found something."

Jake was already having to kneel to avoid banging his head against the ceiling. He awkwardly crab walked across to her. She played her light again.

"See, that glint."

"I see it." He started to move towards it. "Shine the light again."
Obligingly she shone the light on the spot where she had seen the
glint. She moved carefully towards it while keeping the beam
focused on it.

"Ouch." Intent on the spot, she had forgotten the roof was dropping
and had walked into a lower outcropping. "That hurt." She could
feel something start to drip. Touching her forehead, she found she
had cut it, and it had started to bleed.

"Dammit." She pulled a Kleenex from her pocket to wipe it up and
apply pressure.

"Are you okay?" Jake turned towards her.

"No, but I will be. I just cut my head on a rock and it's bleeding."

"Look at this." Jake turned away and was gesturing at her to look at
the wall. A bit piqued at how quickly he had dismissed her injury,
Rachel took her time carefully maneuvering her way over.

On the wall, a small pattern had been carved. The glint of light had
come from a rock embedded in the wall which had clearly been
polished by the carving and despite the years of dust, continued to
gleam faintly through the dirt.

Jake rubbed the dirt away with the palm of his hand.

The pattern became clearer. Two lines started in parallel and
gradually curved closer to one another until they almost touched
and then quickly turned back out from each other to form mirror
image curly Qs.

"What do you think that is?"

Jake shook his head. "I have no idea."

He took off his backpack and pulled out a sheet of paper. Carefully laying it over the pattern he used the side of a pencil to rub back and forth creating an image of the carving on the paper. He started to fold up the paper to put it away.

"Shhhh." Rachel's fingers closed like a vice around his arm. Jake froze. "I thought I heard something."

They both switched off their lights and stood in almost complete darkness. The opening of the cave was a slightly less dark area. Rachel could see two or three stars through it but they weren't enough to provide any light. They stood still barely breathing. The silence lay heavy around them and Jake wasn't sure he would hear anything over the pounding of his heart. But then, a faint clatter. The same clatter that they had made on their way up the hill. The kind of clatter that pebbles make when they are disturbed and tumble down a slope.

"Someone is out there," Rachel whispered fiercely. "What are we going to do?"

"Relax, it could be an animal." Silence once again.

Then, more clatter followed by a faint click. It wasn't an animal. A dim glow barely illuminated the opening but it was enough that both Jake and Rachel knew that a flashlight had been turned on. Jake figured that the person or persons out there knew that he and Rachel were trapped, so he had nothing to lose by turning on a flashlight. In fact, given they had been standing in complete darkness for several minutes, the flashlight would now render them blind and helpless. He stuffed the paper in his back pocket and switched on his flashlight.

"Give me your water bottle." Jake gestured to her canteen.

Already on his knees, he started to pull some dirt in towards him building a little pile.

Rachel handed him the water and he poured it onto the pile trying to mix it into mud.

"What are you doing?" Even in a whisper, her voice squeaked. "We are trapped in this cave with a dangerous man or two or maybe three just outside. Men we know are willing to do just about anything to stop us and you are making mud pies???"

He had made a significant amount of mud.

"Here", he slapped some of it into her hand. "Smear it on the pattern and on other parts of the wall. It might keep them from finding the pattern or at least will slow them down a bit."

He grabbed a couple of handfuls and started to smear it over the wall on his side. She quickly covered the carving and continued to cover her side.

The light gradually became stronger and they knew that whoever it was was moving closer and closer to the cave.

"Take this." Jake thrust his backpack into her hands. "Get ready and when it happens, run. Don't turn around, just run. Get to the car and get out of here."

Suddenly more afraid for him than for herself, she turned to him. "When what happens? What are you going to do, aren't you coming with me? You can't stay here."

"Don't worry; I will be right behind you." He gave her a quick hard hug to reassure and kissed the scrape on her forehead. "Make sure you get that looked after later."

Rachel stood there clutching his pack staring at him. Her eyes were wide with fear. What was he going to do? Why was he telling her to run?

Suddenly Jake yelled, "NOW!"

He launched himself towards the opening where at that very moment a figure became visible, their position marked by the flashlight they held. With a thud, Jake caught the figure right in the ribcage with his shoulder knocking the breath from the shadow with a grunt. Jake's momentum launched them backward. The intruder lost his footing and was unable to move quickly enough to get it back. Jake was at the mercy of his momentum. With the intruder still locked in his grip, they fell. The dry dirt and pebbles gave way under their tumbling bodies and started down the hill in a small avalanche.

Rachel had watched him fall with horror. One moment he was there and then the next he was gone. She could hear the thuds and groans as they rolled down the hillside. She rushed to the opening but couldn't see anything in the dark. Gingerly she made her way to the edge over which they had fallen, not wanting to be a victim as well. She could see the flashlight tumble over and over, sometimes visible, other times not, until it suddenly stopped abruptly at the bottom of the slope.

She realized that if either he or she had a chance, she needed to follow him down the side of the hill to help him to the car. Quickly she shrugged his backpack onto her shoulders. Grateful that there didn't seem to be a second assailant, she concentrated on moving swiftly. The footing was slippery with shale and dirt breaking off and sliding with only the slightest pressure from her feet. She slipped and grabbed randomly for a shrub nearby. It slowed her slide but she felt the roughness of the bark abrade her palm as it too slid through her grasp. She tried to slow down a bit more but even with this effort, she tripped over a stone and landed on her hands and knees. Feeling the pebbles and rocks biting into her knees and hands, she couldn't imagine what Jake had gone through rolling down the hillside.

"Hurry, hurry, hurry," she chanted as she pushed herself back onto her feet.

She reached the bottom and started running towards the light. She prayed that whatever else, the flashlight had followed them down along the same path otherwise she wouldn't be able to find them easily. She wasn't even sure that the two of them would still be together at the bottom as they had been at the top. To her relief, as she drew closer she could see that the mound of people was too big for one person. She skidded to a stop beside them, almost falling onto them.

"Jake, Jake, are you all right?"

Jake lay half under the same swarthy man that had been one of the two in the little green car. Both of them were covered with dust and blood. Rachel wasn't sure whose blood it was but her heart stopped at the sight of it. She didn't know how to check for a pulse but put her hand in front of Jake's mouth. She could feel his breath. "Thank you, God." At least she knew he wasn't dead.

"Jake." She pushed the intruder but found she couldn't shift him off. He was completely limp. Crying, she struggled up to move to his feet. The backpack was heavy and impeded her movements. She pulled it off her shoulders and tossed it aside. She picked the attacker's feet up at the ankles and started to pull. He moved a couple of inches and then she wasn't able to shift him anymore. "Come on, you stupid, stupid man. Get off Jake." Finally, she was able to roll him off Jake by sitting down and using her legs to push him off. She didn't really care if he was hurt and she didn't think that what she was doing was going to hurt him more. Getting to Jake was the priority.

Jake was starting to moan as the man rolled off him.

"Jake, Jake, can you hear me?" Rachel cupped his face in her hands. His face was covered with dirt. He was bleeding from a gash over his right eyebrow. His left eye was beginning to swell. His cheeks and chin were red and bleeding from scratches. His new shirt and jeans were now torn, dirty and bloodstained. She used her shoulder to dash her tears from her eyes. "Jake…"

"What happened?"

Rachel almost broke down with relief. He was conscious and talking. She knew that they needed to get away before the other one regained consciousness too.

"Come on, Jake, you fell. We need to get out of here." She tugged on his hand.

"My head hurts."

"I'm sure it does but we need to get out of here. You can have all the Tylenol and Advil you want when we get back to the hotel." Vainly she tugged again at his hand. He pulled it away.

"Just let me lie here." Jake lay on the ground with his eyes closed. Under the layers of blood and dust, he was completely white. Rachel tried not to think of all the horrible things that could be wrong with him after that fall down the hill. She looked around to gauge the distance to the car. It was then that she realized that in their fall, they had tumbled down the side of the slope that was behind the restaurant and that the car was actually quite far away. She knew that Jake wouldn't be able to walk that far even with her assistance.

"Okay but only for a few minutes. I have to go get the car." Rachel searched his pockets for the key, biting her lip until she found it. She wasn't sure what she would have done if she couldn't find it. That would have meant he lost it in the tumble down the hill.

Pushing herself to her feet she started to jog towards the car. Parking at the watch tower had seemed like a good idea at the time but now it was all up hill. Breathing raggedly by the time she got there, she shoved the key in the lock.

"Come on, come on." She adjusted the seat rapidly and started back down the hill to the parking lot. She was consumed by the fear that the intruder would regain consciousness before she got back and that Jake would be, for all intents and purposes, defenseless. She drove as quickly as she dared down the dark road to the lower parking lot and drove as close as she could to where she had left Jake. Jake was lying where she had left him and the other man hadn't moved.

"Can you move your feet? Come on Jake, move your feet." Rachel had never been so happy to see feet move. "Okay, come on, time to get up." She slid her arm under his shoulders and heaved. "You know you are really heavy." Angling her body to be able to use her legs as braces, she was able to sit him up.

"I don't feel good." He rolled onto his hands and knees. For a moment she thought he might pass out again but he just rested his head on the ground.

"I'm not surprised. But there is no rest for the wicked right now." She tried to heave him to his feet. To her surprise, he started to help. Finally, she had him on his feet although he was still leaning very heavily on her. She glanced at the other body. She hadn't checked to see if he was still alive or not.

"Okay Jake, one step at a time." After what seemed like an eternity, they reached the car. Rachel carefully helped him into the front passenger seat. She tilted the seat back slightly to allow Jake to recline a bit. To steady herself, she thought of how difficult getting the mix of dirt and blood out of the rental car upholstery was going to be. "You just sit here. I'll be right back."

"Okay," Jake leaned his head back and closed his eyes. She couldn't tell if he was simply resting or had passed out again. Either way, she needed to get the backpack.

Quickly she ran back to the bottom of the hill. The backpack was there where she had tossed it and just beyond that, she could see the mound of the other man. She scooped up the backpack and turned back to the car. She hesitated. She started to trot back the car and then stopped. She looked back at the dark lump on the ground. She wondered if she should check to see if he was okay or not. She couldn't do it. She turned and ran back to the car.

Faced with the task of getting them back to the ferry and from there to their hotel, Rachel wanted to break down and cry. While she had been grateful that Jake had done all the driving before, she now thought that she should have done some. She had to drive on the opposite side of the road, in the dark and without an navigator. Briefly she rested her head on the steering wheel fighting the urge to dissolve into tears. She was better than that. Jake needed her to get him out of there. So that was what she would do. Sniffing back her tears and hardening her resolve, she started the car and put it into gear.

Fortunately, because it was relatively late and the spot where they had been was reasonably remote from the closest town, there initially wasn't a lot of traffic. She got used to driving on the opposite side and simply kept chanting to herself, 'I'm in the middle', to keep herself in the left hand lane. She made a couple of mistakes getting around the corners but for the most part was feeling better by the time she hit the outskirts of town. Once there she was able to simply follow the car in front of her as well as the signs to the ferry. As a tourist spot, it was well marked so she was able to find it easily. Pulling onto the ferry, she heaved a huge sigh of relief. If she had made it that far, she could get them the rest of the way back to the hotel.

18

Jake groaned and pulled the duvet over his eyes. The sun through the crack in the curtains felt like a jackknife into his eyeballs. His head felt like it was going to pound off his shoulders. And, at this point, he would be fine with that. He groaned again and tried to roll away from the light.

"Ouch, what the...." He could feel parts of his skin sticking to the sheets and as he rolled, the sheet tore off creating burning pain that seemed to come from all parts of his body.

He lifted himself up on his elbows and tried to focus. He was lying in his bed in his underwear and everywhere he could see seemed to be either black and blue with bruising or red with scrapes and cuts. Some of the cuts were starting to ooze fresh blood where he had torn the scabs off with the sheet.

"What happened?" He tried to sit but was overcome with a wave of dizziness. He sank back into the pillows and closed his eyes. There was no hurry, he rationalized. He didn't have to get up. He would try again in a few minutes. Until then he would try and figure out why he was lying in his bed with a pounding headache, looking like he had been beaten.

He replayed the events of the day before. He and Rachel had headed over to Gozo. They had arrived just fine and had been able to find the Azure Window with no problems. Lunch, wandering over the rocks, looking for a hiding place or a cave or something. A cave, he focused his thoughts, a cave. They had found a cave and had decided to wait until dark before exploring it. It had been up a bit of a climb but it had looked like the most likely spot to search. He remembered the climb and then how the cave started out big enough to stand up in, but then he had had to get on his knees. He concentrated. A flash of memory. Another person. Making mud. Flying through the air and then rolling and rolling and…after that, it was a blank. He started to sit up again just as a knock sounded on his door.

He swung his legs over the edge of the bed and then held on as the room seemed to swing in the opposite direction and then up and down. His door opened and Rachel stuck her head in.

"Hi there, sleepyhead." Rachel tried not to let her immense relief be seen on her face. She had brought him back the night before and had tried to clean him up as best she could. She had stripped off his shirt and pants and had been hoping to get him into the shower when he had passed out again. Luckily he had fallen onto the bed enough she had been able to lift his legs up and settle him in. She had washed and cleaned the scrapes as best she could. She had made icepacks for his eye and some of the worst bruises. The entire time she had been praying frantically that there wouldn't be anything more serious wrong with him. He had seemed to be sleeping rather than unconscious by the time she had made up a bed on the floor for herself. But he had been sleeping for hours and she had started to get worried. She had roused him a bit before she had left but he had still seemed pretty out of it. She had gone out for coffee and to buy more Band-Aids and antibiotic cream, promising herself that if he wasn't awake by the time she came back, she would call an ambulance.

"Here," she handed him a glass of water and two painkillers. "I imagine you have a headache and are a little sore. These should help."

"Thanks," he swallowed the pills almost choking in his eagerness to get something into him that would calm the raging pain.

Rachel fluffed up the pillows at the head of the bed. "Lie back for a few minutes and let the pills do their work."

Grateful, he sank back into the softness. "Rachel, can you tell me what happened? I remember going to Gozo and then looking at a cave we were going to search." He shook his head and immediately wished he hadn't. "But after that it is pretty much a blur. The next thing I really remember is waking up here, and given my headache, wishing that I hadn't woken up."

Rachel pulled a chair up beside the bed where he wouldn't have to strain to see her. She reached for his hand to hold, as much to make herself feel better as to comfort him. "I'm not surprised you don't remember parts of it. You had a bad tumble and you were unconscious for a while. I'm pretty sure you have a concussion. We started searching the cave, do you remember that?"

Eyes closed, he shook his head and then winced as the pounding doubled. "No, I just remember getting to the cave."

"Well, we were able to get to the cave without too much bother. You started from one side and I started from the other side and we were going to meet in the middle at the back. But I found something on the wall that looked like it had been carved. We made an etching from it and just as we finished we could hear someone. They made it to the mouth of the cave and then you went rushing toward them. The two of you ended up rolling down the hillside to the very bottom. By the time I got there, you were unconscious but you came around pretty quickly. I was able to get you into the car and back to the hotel. With my support, you were able to walk to your room. Fortunately, we were able to sneak through the lobby without anyone seeing us." She coloured slightly. "I undressed you, but before you could take a shower, you collapsed again. So I had to give you a bed bath to clean the scrapes. You have been asleep ever since."

He looked down at his bare chest and grinned. "I wondered how that had happened. Usually, if I lose my shirt I remember the event!" He chuckled at her discomfort.

"Did we manage to keep the etching?"
Rachel nodded and walked over to the desk. She picked up a sheet of paper and brought it to him. "I couldn't sleep after all of that last night so I spent several hours trying to figure out what it might be." She shrugged, disappointed. "I can come up with a long list of things it might be but can't figure out what it is."

Jake started at the rough outline of the design. Suddenly, a thought struck him.

"Rachel, if that guy found us, what is going to stop him or his boss from finding the mark in the cave?"

She perched on the chair. "You told me to make mud with our water and the dirt on the floor and to smear it on the cave walls. I tried to cover the carving as well as other parts at random. It may not be much but hopefully, it will either keep them from finding it or at least slow them down a bit." She bit her lip. "Besides, I'm not really sure how the other guy was. I didn't go and check on him to make sure he was okay. Once I got him off you, I was more worried about you and getting you back here in case you were really badly injured." Her eyes filled with tears. "I know I probably should have checked better, but I was too scared that he might come after us again."

Jake reached out to grip her hand. "Hey, it's all right. I'm sure he was okay. Besides, the bad guys seem to be able to communicate with each other, so he was probably able to call for help, or they would have come looking for him pretty quickly. It was better and safer for you to get us out of there. You did the right thing." He paused. She still looked worried. "I'll tell you what. First we'll check on line to see if there is anything reported and if not, we will buy a couple of newspapers and see if we can find any news reports about an accident out by the Azure Window. Okay? If he was injured or worse, then he would have been found and it would be in the media."

Rachel nodded, wiped her eyes and blew her nose.

"Besides, I am simply grateful and impressed that you were able to get us out of there and back here in one piece. That must have been quite the adventure for you. Is the car okay?" He grinned at her.

More settled she gave a wry smile in return. "The car is just fine, thank you very much for your display of confidence. I'd like to say it was no problem but, well, it was pretty stressful."

She sat up straighter and squared her shoulders, trying to regain her composure.

"All right. Maybe you will have better luck figuring out what this squiggle means."

19

Jake looked at the drawing and turned it up and down. Regardless of how he looked at it, it made no sense to him. The medication had helped but his head was still pounding. He lay back against the pillows and closed his eyes.

"What's the clue in the journal?" he asked. "Maybe we need to look at this in the context of the clue rather than just on its own."

Rachel gingerly opened the journal to the final pages. "The last clue in the journal reads 'Eight points on the cross, the tired and heavily burdened seek safety from the arrows of their enemies, and water for their thirst.'" She looked up. "Mean anything to you?"

Jake wearily shook his head. "No. But let's break it down."

Rachel looked at him with concern. His colour wasn't good and the bruising had continued to develop over night so the purplish marks now stood in stark contrast to the paleness of his skin.

"Jake, we can do this later. You need to rest." Rachel closed the book and set it aside.

"I'm okay, Rachel. I just have a headache." He opened his eyes as best he could, given one was swollen almost completely shut, and summoned up a reassuring smile. "You are the historian so where would they have gone to seek safety?"

Rachel gave him another sharp look. "If you are sure."

"I'm sure."

"Safety would have been found within the walls of any walled city like Valletta. And of course, in the tunnels beneath the city as well. Some of the buildings would have been reinforced to withstand fighting in case the city fell to the enemy during a siege."

"I don't think that he would have used the tunnels twice, although I suppose nothing is impossible." Jake said. "Is Valletta the only walled city on Malta?"

Rachel thought for a moment. "No, Mdina is another walled city. It is located more inland and on top of a hill which made it very defensible. And," Rachel's voice lifted with excitement. "And, it's the only city on the island which was built in such a way that each street curves almost continuously. As one walks, there is less that one arrow's path of visibility. That meant in the case of an invasion, if the invaders breached the city, arrows were useless as weapons. The road would turn before the arrow completed its flight. The residents were able to flee and the walls kept them safe." She stood up and started to pace around the room. "I can't believe I had forgotten that. I have always thought that it must have been an engineering nightmare to design and build such a place."

Jake smiled at her genuine distress that she had forgotten about this unique city. "I am pretty sure you had some other things to worry about, Rachel. But, it sounds as if Medina is the place we need to go." He carefully sat up and swung his legs out of the bed. Wincing, he carefully stood. Finding that he was able to do that without a problem, he started to make his way to the bathroom. "I'll take a shower and then we can have a bite to eat before going to Medina."

"Em-dina." said Rachel.

"What?" Jake stopped on his way across the room.

"Em-dina is how it is pronounced. Most people think it is Medina but it is Mdina."

"Oh, okay. Mdina."

Rachel had left Jake and had gone back to her own room to shower and change her clothes herself. It had taken a while for Jake to be able to get himself ready and he found that he was more ready for a nap than a trip to another city by the time he was done. Rachel was in no hurry to drive again, especially during busier traffic, so they opted to take a taxi.

During the drive from Valletta, Rachel had given Jake a condensed history lesson on the city. Mdina was 'the city' and adjacent to it was Rabat, also known as 'the suburb'. Rabat's claim in history was the grotto where St Paul had stayed for several months after being shipwrecked on Malta on his way to Rome. It was from those caves that he had started the fledgling Christian church on Malta. The grotto had been located in a ditch just outside of the city. Over time, that area had also come to host many catacombs which had significant for both pagans and Christians.

The taxi let them out at the main gate of Mdina. The city, much older than Valletta, was, as Rachel had described, walled and set on the summit of a hill. The main street was large enough for a vehicle but most of the side streets were too narrow for any cars. The buildings rose up two to three stories and cast a shadow over the adjacent streets. This kept the atmosphere cool and comfortable. As they walked, it was easy to see evidence of the unique feature of Mdina.

Rachel found that the constant turning of the roads made for a very romantic city. The city revealed itself in stages as one walked. Each street slowly unwound to display its pleasures one by one. The walls along the streets were regularly punctuated by overly tall double doors. Each set of doors had matching brass door knockers. Themes of lions, the Maltese cross and fish were repeated throughout the city. Rachel thought it was likely that many of the doors hid courtyards behind them. The height of the doors would have allowed a mounted rider to enter the yard without having to dismount first.

They gave themselves time to simply slowly wander the city. As they walked, Jake felt himself starting to recover some of his strength. The angled streets were to Jake and Rachel's advantage as they would be able to identify followers. To be able to follow effectively, they would have to stay close enough that they would be easily spotted. They climbed onto the ramparts to enjoy the view of the surrounding valley. Finally, they found a small café in one of the lovely squares, Piazza Mesquita, where they settled for a late afternoon snack and coffee. Jake purchased three of the local newspapers which published English editions. Despite having found nothing about an injured man or problems at the Azure window after searching online before leaving the hotel, Jack thought it was worth checking the news the old fashioned way.

Rachel anxiously leafed through one of them. There was no article about an injured man or any incident at the Azure Window that she was able to find. Jake similarly found nothing. She sighed with relief and sat back in her chair.

"Funny how after they have intended to harm us in the past, I was so worried about one of them."

"That's what makes you different than them. That's also why you would never steal artifacts for yourself or the black market."

"Well, now that that is settled, on to the next clue. The safety from arrows has brought us to Mdina, assuming that we have interpreted that correctly." Rachel paused. "The tired and heavily burden, we aren't sure of the significance of that and the thirst comment would seem to point towards a well or source of water. Do you think the etching we found is a mark that we will match on a particular well?" Horrified by a sudden thought, she sat up straight almost spilling the table over. "What happens if they have filled in whatever well he might have been talking about. What if it went dry? Or now that they have running water they don't need a well and so they blocked it up to prevent kids from falling in? What if they unknowingly buried hidden treasure?"

Jake was feeling very serene at this point. His eye was still puffy and he had various aches and pains over his body. Different areas seem to flare to his attention at different times. His incredible good fortune from the events of last night made it a bit easier to be philosophical. He carefully mopped up coffee that Rachel had spilled. "Well, no pun intended, if it has been filled in, then we are likely going to be out of luck."

"Well, no time like the present. There is a well right over there. I am going to go take a look." Rachel pushed up from her chair and walked across the piazza.

Jake only admired the view of her well shaped back as she moved away from him.

At the well, Rachel looked carefully on the stones making up the mouth. They rose four stone widths above the ground. On the outside she could see no markings of any sort. The mouth itself had been covered over with plywood but what she could see of the inside of the well had again, nothing. No inscriptions, no markings, nothing to indicate that the well was anything out of the ordinary. She turned her attention to the iron bars which made up what she assumed, would have been the support for the bucket. It appeared old but was in good condition. There were four posts which stood about five feet tall demarcating each quarter of the circle. Each rod had a flat iron piece attached with a loop. They then curved up towards the center point formed by all four pieces. A central part held them all together. Rachel marveled at the work it would have taken to hammer out each piece. And each piece, while slightly different, was essentially the same as the matching three others. The curve of the arch from post to center was the same. The width of the piece was the same. From the central portion, each of the four slats was bent up straight and then curled around back on themselves. A small cross topped the entire fixture. Rachel fished the copy of the etching out of her purse. If she turned it upside down, the etching they had fit the curly q's. There hadn't been a cross on the wall of the cave that she could remember. She wondered now, though, if they had missed it in the stress of hearing the intruder coming. Trying to contain her excitement, she walked quickly back to Jake. Could it really be that the first well she looked at was the one they wanted? Could it really be that easy? It was hard to believe that it might be the case.

"Look at this." She held the picture upside down for him to see. "Add a cross on the top of that picture and what do you get?" She motioned towards the well behind her with her head.

Jake blinked to try to clear the blurriness from his left eye. The swelling made it difficult for him to focus. "Well, I see what you are saying. It fits if we add in the cross. But none of the other clues required us to 'add in' things. They were all pretty complete in their own right. Why would he have made this one any different?"

Rachel folded the paper and put it away. "Maybe we missed the cross. Maybe he didn't add the cross because he didn't want to be too obvious. It seems like this is the last spot so if it is where he hid the treasure, he might have wanted people to second guess themselves. Or maybe, he didn't have time to finish the carving. Maybe he was interrupted as we were. Or maybe this isn't the right place."

Jake looked doubtful. "That's a lot of maybes."

"Maybe so, but I am going to look down that well tonight." Rachel could feel that this was the right spot. After all their searching, all their traveling over the island and all their close calls, this was the place. A frisson of electric excitement shot through her. Could this actually be happening?

After finishing their snack, they had roamed the city waiting for sunset. Jake found that the walking helped to ease the pain from the bruises as well as loosen up his muscles. They had visited the cathedral, walked down into the depths of the cliffs to visit St Paul's Grotto and had even stopped at a local hardware store to pick up some sturdy rope. As Jake said to Rachel, there was no way that either of them would be going down the well if they didn't have rope. During their wanderings, they had kept an eye out for other wells or sources of water. They weren't able to find anything that even loosely fit the etching. Finally, the café closed, the streets cleared of people traveling home from work and darkness fell.

Jake was pretty sure that they hadn't been followed at all but insisted that they do a quick walk around the area again to ensure that there was no one loitering. Rachel's excitement was growing and even Jake could feel himself starting to feel the thrill of the chase.

They returned to the centre of the courtyard and in the dim lamp light which lit the area, they carefully looked at the fixture over the well. Each post was solidly embedded in the wall of the well. Jake stood on the edge to inspect the soldering at the top of the structure. It too appeared stable.

He hopped down. "Well, they did good work back in the 1500's. It looks super solid. I guess maybe that is why they left it up."

They turned their attention to the plywood covering the mouth of the well. It had been set down into the mouth several inches. It was made up of two halves which had been placed into an area of the well which was a bit wider and then fastened together with a board across the seam. Jake wasn't entirely sure how they had been able to do that but it was certainly effective. Because it sat in a wider section, they wouldn't be able to simply lift or pry it off the well. It wouldn't fit through. They were left with having to take the central board off and removing the cover piece by piece.

Rachel looked defeated. "Damn, how are we going to get that off? It looks too new for us to be able to break it. And I don't think that we can pry it off."

Jake pulled out his Swiss army knife. "Boy Scouts to the rescue. I am prepared." He pulled out the screwdriver from the knife. Luckily the screws that had been used were the same size Philips head as his knife carried.

It was laborious work. Whoever had put the lid together had wanted to be sure that the cover stayed put. They took turns unscrewing the long screws that had been used. The knife was small so it was a difficult task to get each one out but finally, they were down to the last one.

"Carefully now. Rachel, can you slide your fingers under the center piece and hold one of the plywood halves? I want to be able to put this back together again when we are done so I don't want to lose a piece down the well if we can help it."

Rachel squiggled her fingers under the crosspiece. She was just able to get her fingers onto the one-half. "All I can do is push it against the wall. It is too heavy for me to hold."

"That's fine," said Jake. "as long as you can push it in hard enough to keep it from falling, I will get the other one out and then rescue you."

Jake slowly unscrewed the remaining screw. As soon as he felt it pop through the one board, he lifted off the center piece and one half of the lid without waiting to completely remove the cross piece. Quickly he turned back to Rachel and caught the other side, just as it was beginning to tilt into the well. A loose screw sitting on top of it rolled to the edge and fell. After what seemed like a long time, they both heard a faint splash.

"There is still water in there and it seems to be a fair way down. Are you sure you want to do this?" Jake asked Rachel.

"Me? I'm going to get to go down?" Rachel was surprised but delighted.

"Why not? This is your moment. You knew from the beginning that there was treasure to be had. Besides, you are lighter than me and while I think the iron work is in great shape, it doesn't hurt to be cautious. I will be your counterweight in case there is a problem."

Rachel practically danced over to him and gave him a kiss on the mouth and a hug. "Thank you, thank you. I thought you were going to do the 'it's too dangerous' routine."
She paused. "Are you sure you will be okay holding on to me? You must still be pretty sore from last night."

Jake waved off her concern. "I'm fine."

They fashioned a harness for her which allowed her to partially sit as she rappelled her way down. Jake strung the rope up over the top of the iron posts formed by the curly q's and made sure that it was able to move smoothly. He took his shirt off and used it to protect his hands as he hadn't thought to bring gloves. Why he would have thought of that as they left for a day of walking around Mdina, he had no idea but apparently, when one was with Rachel, one needed to be prepared for anything and everything.

Rachel stepped over the edge and planted her feet on the side of the well. The roughness of the wall and her rubber soles gave her good purchase. She started to move down the well.

"Wait, you are going to need these." Jake handed her the flashlight and his Swiss army knife. "Well, you might not need the knife but at least you will have it." He bent over and gave her a kiss for good luck. He lingered over it, feeling her soft lips under his. He opened his eyes without moving away. "Be careful." She looked at him, eyes shining with excitement.

"I will."

She slowly began her descent. She started a pattern of moving down a couple of feet and then rotating around the entire well to examine each part of the wall. She used Jake's position to mark the beginning and the end of her circle.

The stones were large blocks, more the size of cement blocks than regular bricks. The humidity from the water had allowed slime and algae to grow over the surface of the stone making her footing treacherous. As she moved deeper, the smell of stagnant water became more dominant. She started to breathe through her mouth.

She completed three circles and slowly moved down to her next stop. She felt a bit of a catch on the rope but then it started to slide more easily again.

She moved her feet side to side carefully. She made sure that she looked at every inch of stone. In some places, the algae were starting to grow more thickly, so she had to scrape it away with her shoe. She had seen nothing but stone. Each stone looked similar to the one before. This time as she started to scrape, her shoe caught on an edge. Excitement flashed through her. She played the flashlight over the area. Could it be? She began to rub more quickly and sure enough, a pattern became evident. In the very center of the stone was etched what had originally been the Amalfi Cross but had become known as the Maltese Cross. It was the symbol worn by all Knights and had to be the 8 pointed cross in the clue.

"Jake, Jake," Her voice echoed up and down the well.

Jake's face appeared as a pale oval at the top of the well. "Did you find something?"

"There's a stone with the Maltese cross on it." Rachel could barely open the Swiss army knife in her excitement. Her hands were sweating and she almost dropped it. She grabbed it and held on. She forced herself to slow down and take a deep breath. She called up to Jake. "I'm going to move over towards the marked stone. Is that okay for you?"

Jake had been feeding the rope out when she moved down and then holding it when she did her circuit. He was a bit concerned about the fact that it had caught once but on the whole, it seemed to be working well. He was very glad he had sacrificed his shirt for the operation as he was sure that his hands would have been shredded by now. He was sore in a lot of places but that wasn't affecting his ability to hold her.

He planted his feet more firmly on the side of the well. "Go for it," he called sotto voice over the edge of the well. He had had time to look around the square while he had been standing there and he was glad that it appeared to be mostly commercial. He wasn't sure what he would say if someone came along. He figured he could pretend to be a city worker but not speaking Maltese would likely end that subterfuge pretty quickly. He stuck with praying that no one would come by.

Rachel worked herself so that she was positioned beside the stone. It looked as if it were pretty solidly in place. Carefully, she used the knife to try to scrape out the mortar between it and its neighbors. The first few millimeters of mortar were pretty hard and she had trouble getting it out. After that, it seemed to become more sand like and was easier for her to remove. She began to wonder how thick the stone was. If it was too thick, she wouldn't be able to remove all of the mortar. Finally, she had removed all she could, the longest tool on the knife was now too short to reach the mortar that was left. She banged on the stone in frustration. So close, they were so close. With the second bang, she thought she felt the stone shift.

"Jake," She waited until she could see his face. "I'm going to try swinging back a bit and kicking the stone to dislodge it."

"Okay but make it quick." Jake's arms were beginning to burn from the effort of keeping the rope stable. He could feel Rachel push herself off the wall and then connect with the other side. The iron groaned ominously.

"It worked." He heard her excited exclamation. "I'm going to try one more time."

The strain on his arms was becoming acute. He was beginning to feel every bump and bruise from his tumble. "Rachel, you'll have to hurry. I can't hold you for much longer."

Rachel vaguely heard Jake speaking. But all of her attention was focused on the gleam she could see coming from behind the wall of the well. Her last swing had shifted the stone so that it was turned sideways. She shone the flashlight into the gap. Behind the wall of the well was an area which had obviously been excavated on purpose. It wasn't huge but she was unable to see exactly how far back it reached. Within the cave, were what looked like dozens of items. Some had been wrapped in oilskin or cloth; some were sitting in the open. She could see silver plates and goblets, silver cutlery tumbled together with serving spoons. Several more elaborate goblets, carved and impressed with precious jewels were visible. A small wooden box which had decayed and broken open revealed several large rings of silver and gold with precious stones inlaid. Judging from the size of the oilskin packages, some were likely books and others might be paintings. Rachel carefully reached inside to remove some of the closest objects. She tucked two into her shirt. Using her feet again, she tried to shove the displaced stone back into position. Trying to get leverage, she pushed back from the wall and braced herself with one foot. The other she banged against the corner of the stone shifting it by inches back into its position. Carefully, she finished maneuvering it in as closely as she could. She didn't want to push it too hard as she didn't want it to fall into the space behind. Suddenly, Jake yelled and at the same time she felt something give way and she began to fall. She braced her feet against one side and her back against the other but the slime simply allowed her to continue her downward slide. She pushed harder and slowly her fall stopped. Her heart was pounding like a jackhammer and she no longer noticed the rancid smell as she breathed rapidly.

"Jake? Are you all right?" Her voice reverberated off the walls and was loud in her ears. She could barely hear his response but felt the upward tug of the rope around her waist. Working as quickly as she could, she braced herself again and tried to work her way back up. The slide had scraped much of the slime off the wall so she was better able to plant herself as she moved up the well. At the level of the marked stone, she took care not to put any pressure on the wall. She could feel Jake taking up the slack as she created it.

Finally reaching the surface, Jake pulled her out. Both of them collapsed on the ground leaning against the well, trying to catch their breath.

"What happened? Are you okay?" Rachel asked Jake.

Wordlessly Jake showed her the rope. The friction generated as she had circled the well had worn through several strands of the rope. When they had given way, Jake had lost his grip and she had fallen until he was able to get it back. Rachel paled at the thought of what might have happened. She took Jake's hands and turned them over. The shirt had protected them somewhat but he had been more concerned with keeping her from falling that protecting his hands. His palms were abraded and bloody from rope burn. Rachel bent her head and kissed each palm gently. She then reached into her shirt and pulled out a gold cross, intricately carved and set with emeralds. She laid it on his left palm. She then removed a silver cup inscribed with the Knights' motto 'Pro Fide, Pro Utilitate Hominum' and placed it in his other hand. Jake stared at them with disbelief.

"We found it. It actually exists and we found it."

Rachel bit her lower lip to keep the tears from spilling over. "We did."

Epilogue

Jake and Rachel stood hand in hand watching a steady stream of people wander through the most recent, most revered display in the Grand Master's Palace. As they stood there, Jake thought about all that had taken place over the past six months.

The day after they had made their trip down the well, Jake and Rachel had gone to the authorities and explained the entire situation. It had taken several hours and several times through the story, producing the journal, admitting to defacing the tunnels with lipstick (for which they had eventually been forgiven), going through the clues and the photos, and basically working through their entire adventure before the police had concluded that they had been working for the good of the treasure, and that they weren't bad guys.

It wasn't until the next day when they had seen front page headlines announcing the arrest of a visiting history professor and two members of the local criminal crowd, that they had understood why they had been interrogated as they had. The same night they had been investigating the well, police had received a phone call that there were some strange lights on a hillside at the Azure Window. Expecting partying young people, they had stumbled upon Dr. Bothell and his two muscle men in the cave. Dr. Bothell was standing observing while one of the men jackhammered the floor of the cave. When the professor had tried to claim that he was merely an innocent bystander who had been forced into helping the two criminals in their search, the men had decided the save themselves. They had quickly told police about all of their illegal activities including stalking Jake and Rachel, shooting at them, and ransacking Jake's room. They could not tell the story fast enough to ensure that all the blame for what they did fell at the feet of Dr. Bothell. Given the police knew that they were local petty criminals, it had not been difficult to believe that they had simply been hired muscle. Rachel had taken pleasure in seeing the photo of all three of the men led from the cave in handcuffs. It hadn't been long after that, that the university had uncovered more of the professor's black market activities. A search of his home had resulted in a substantial number of artifacts being recovered. He had also kept meticulous records of what artifacts and to whom he had sold them. He had been stripped of his university position and was headed for a long stretch in a Maltese prison. After that, there were several other countries waiting to extradite him for their chance to prosecute.

Jake and Rachel had been invited to witness the excavation of the treasure. At that time, the seemingly irrelevant part of the last clue, the eight points of the cross, had been revealed. The stone marking the site of the treasure was eight stones from the top. The authorities had set up a more stable scaffolding and had spent several hours enlarging the hole that Rachel had made and slowly retrieving artifacts. Rachel helped to catalog them and now had an open invitation to visit and study them anytime she desired. She had helped to curate the permanent exhibit of artifacts of the Knights' Hospitaller in the Grand Place. They had entitled it 'The Lost Treasure of Malta.'

"Fantastic display, my son." Jake's father had flown in for the opening of the exhibit. "I can't believe that our ancestor and his friends did all of this." He shook his head. "What a marvelous gift you have given Malta. I am so proud of both of you." He shook Jake's hand and gave him a back-slapping hug. Rachel received a proper hug and kiss on the cheek. "So, when's the wedding?"

"Dad!" Exasperated, Jake punched his dad in the shoulder. He turned to Rachel, "But I do think that is an excellent idea. So, Dr.

Corbyn, shall we get married?"

Rachel smiled her brilliant smile and then laughed. Throwing her arms around him, she exclaimed "Absolutely. As long as you promise me that things won't always be this exciting."

Historical Note

The Sovereign Order of St. John has its roots in a hospital founded in Jerusalem in the eleventh century by a group of monks led by Brother Gerard and funded by merchants from Amalfi. To the Brothers, the hospital was their opportunity to serve the Lord's sick and poor, regardless of religion. For the Amalfi merchants the hospital was key to helping pilgrim to the Holy Land, many of whom arrived sick and injured after the long and difficult journey from Europe. A group of Knights of the First Crusade, upon entering Jerusalem in July 1099, joined in their efforts. The resultant knight/hospitaller organization was recognized as a Sovereign Order by Pascal II in a Papal Bull dated February 15, 1113. During the second Crusade, the Sovereign Order continued the hospitaller traditions, but also became one of the principal defenders of the Latin (Christian) States in the Holy Land.

After the collapse of the Christian Kingdom of Jerusalem in the late thirteenth century, the Sovereign Order of St. John fled to Cyprus where they stayed for 14 years before securing a more permanent base in Rhodes where they ruled for the next two hundred years – continuing their service to the sick and poor but changing from a land based fighting force to the largest Christian naval force in the Mediterranean. Because of their continued threat to the Muslim countries of the eastern Mediterranean, in 1528 Suleiman the Magnificent invaded Rhodes and after a lengthy siege, forced the Order to flee the island. Left without a home, the Knights wandered the Mediterranean until, in 1530 the Holy Roman Emperor, Charles V signed the Act of Donation of Malta bestowing the Island of Malta to the Sovereign Order. The only feudal service demanded in return was the annual payment, on All Saints Day, of a single falcon, which was to be given to Charles Viceroy in Sicily. This annual token payment was the origin of the legend of the Maltese Falcon.

Upon arrival in Malta, the Order instituted a series of changes, welcomed by the local population. Being seafarers rather than a land based society, they established their seat of authority, not in the existing capital of Mdina, an inland city some five miles from the coast, but rather on the southeast coast, building the tri-cities of Birgu, Senglea, and Cospicua. They built the current capital, Valletta, in 1565, across the harbor from the tri-cities. They also built much-needed infrastructure: roads, hospitals and schools, all designed to improve the quality of life for everyone living on the island. Until their arrival the majority of youth had no formal schooling.

While establishing their new headquarters, they continued their sea-based activities, protecting the Christian merchant fleets and small towns and cities around the Mediterranean and harassing the Muslim ships in the area. As a result of their military and hospital service, over the next 200 years the Order amassed great wealth. However, by the late 18th century, the Order had lost some of its original vision and, in part as a result of its amassed fortune, and changing global political realities, had started to lose both its purpose and function. The local population, once very supportive of the Knights, were now feeling oppressed and the Order seemed more focused on celebrating its wealth by building a cathedral to rival the great cathedrals of mainland Europe and hoarding vast quantities of gold, silver and other treasures. Because membership in the Order was dependent on being of noble birth, many of the Knights also had large tracks of land across Europe, especially in France, which they gifted to the Order. These lands generated significant revenues.

This was the context when, in 1798 Napoleon set out conquer Egypt with the largest naval fighting force of the time. Malta, directly in his path, became a strategic asset to be taken. Defeating the Order would not only provide Napoleon with vast amounts of gold and silver to pay his soldiers and sailors, taking over their lands in France would secure long term wealth and stability for his homeland – and be in keeping with his general desire to rid France of the yoke of aristocracy.

The Order was no match for Napoleon. With less than a thousand Knights and a local population no longer supporting them, they had little choice but to surrender. After a few days and only sporadic fighting, the SOSJ handed Malta, all of their treasure and, most important, the rights to their lands in France, to Napoleon. After 260 years the SOSJ was once again, homeless. Worse still, with no Sovereign head, the Order faced extinction. Without a sovereign protector or their own land, the SOSJ would suffer the same fate as their fellow Order, the Knights Templar some 400 years before.

Forced by Napoleon to evacuate Malta, individual Knights dispersed across Europe. While a small group settled in Rome, a much larger group, more than 150 of the remaining Knights, headed to the safety of Russia, where they had been offered protection by Czar Paul 1. The following year these Knights, as per their laws and customs, elected Czar Paul 1 as their Sovereign Grand Master. While this did not sit well with the previous Grand Master who had surrendered to Napoleon, having abdicated his position as part of his surrender, there was nothing he could do.

The Order of St John was, from the very beginning, focused on serving the Lord's sick and poor. Even after it was defeated in Malta people recognized its great value. Thus, while the Sovereign Order focused its energy on expanding through the Russian empire, other Sovereign heads, notably the Pope in 1803 and Queen Victoria in 1850 saw the value of such a body and created their own, equally valid Orders – the Sovereign Military Order of Malta and the Venerable Order of St. John respectively. All of these organizations, and several others bearing the name of St. John, continue to work around the globe serving the Lord's sick and poor.

--Daryl Rock
with research and notes from the Sovereign Order of St John of Jerusalem, Knights Hospitaller, www.sosjinternational.org

About the Author

Melanie Rock is a member of the Sovereign Order of St John of Jerusalem, Ontario Commandery. Born in Windsor, Ontario she spent the first four years of her life in Bermuda where she developed a passion for the sea. Returning to Canada, her family settled in Ottawa, the nation's capital. After graduating from medical school in 1995, Melanie practiced Family Medicine in Ottawa and Vancouver. She is an avid traveler – especially Europe and the Caribbean, voracious reader, loves cooking gourmet meals and enjoys fine wines and bubblies. She was invested in the Order in Malta in 2014 and is an active member of the Ontario Commandery raising funds to support palliative care for the homeless. Writing has long been a passion of hers which a busy career as a physician kept her from pursuing –until now. She currently resides in Vancouver with her husband and two cats.

Made in the USA
Lexington, KY
21 May 2018